HIDDEN
PRIZES

AUDREY CONSTANT

Scripture Union
130 City Road, London EC1V 2NJ.

With grateful thanks to The Fortune Centre of Riding Therapy and the Riding for the Disabled Association for their advice and assistance in the preparation of this book.

By the same author:
Cassie

Phototypeset by Intype, London
Printed and bound in Great Britain by Cox and Wyman Ltd, Reading

For Katharine and Rebecca with my love

~1~

I ran my hand down the mare's foreleg and felt the hot and swollen fetlock. I put the hoof gently down and patted the sleek brown neck. Shelly responded by nuzzling my shoulder.

'It's no good, old girl,' I told her. 'That puts us out of the running for next Saturday.'

It had happened yesterday when, for no particular reason, the mare had landed badly over a small jump. She may not have been giving the matter her full attention but it wasn't the only time lately she had been careless, and if we were to keep up our record in the junior competitions, we couldn't afford to make these mistakes.

Shelly came to us four years ago when I was fourteen and had outgrown my first pony. I had won some top prizes with her in local shows but she couldn't go on for ever. What I needed now was a young horse, one that I could train up to replace her.

Putting a halter over her head, I led her, limping, to the paddock. There was plenty of shade there and she would be all right for the day. I closed the gate and went into breakfast.

The old farmhouse gleamed in the early morning sun. The back door stood wide open and a delicious smell of cooking wafted towards me. I knew Mum had been up early baking cakes for a stall in the local market. Dad had already done two hours work and he and Philip, my younger brother by two years, were tucking into their bacon and eggs.

'How's the mare?' Dad asked as I took my place at the table and poured myself a cup of tea.

I shook my head. 'She won't be right for Saturday, or come to that, for some time. She needs rest. Dad, I've simply got to think about another horse.'

'We've discussed this before. Maybe we could do something about it if you'd set your sights lower, but you're talking about a lot of money and I don't have that much to spare at the moment. I'm sorry, Paula, but you'll just have to wait a little longer.'

I knew how hard it was for Dad at the moment. It hadn't been a good year for farmers and now that beef prices had suddenly dropped, he was going to lose out at a time when he desperately needed the money.

I had been born on the farm and so had Philip – just as Dad had and his father before him. It had been in the family for three generations now, but I had heard Mum and Dad discussing how much longer they would be able to hold on to it. I felt sorry for them, but if I was to carve out a career for myself in the show jumping world, I simply had to replace Shelly this season. I was doing well but competition was keen and it was useless to train up a young horse unless it had the necessary qualities, and that cost money.

'I do understand, Dad,' I said, 'but Shelly's getting on and I must have another horse next year. The cheapest way is to buy a good youngster and train it myself. I've seen just the right colt at Studlands, but he'll cost quite a lot even if Bruce could be persuaded to sell him. Couldn't we borrow some money?'

'Definitely no. I'm up to the hilt as it is. If I present the bank manager with a further request, this time for a horse for my daughter, I can tell you he won't look at it sympathetically.'

'Then I'll go and see him myself,' I said. 'I'll show him my cups and winnings up to date, and they've been pretty good.'

'And after deducting shoeing, vet's bills, food and transport, where's the profit?' My father cut my calculations down to size.

'Dad, that's unfair! The food and hay are here anyway, and the vet only looked at Shelly a couple of times when you'd already called him to treat a cow.'

'All has to be paid for,' said Philip, suddenly breaking in. He looked older than his sixteen years and took after Mum with his thick reddish hair and brown eyes, while my hair was long and fair and my eyes were a deep blue, like Dad's. Neither Phil nor I had inherited Mum's gentle, placid character. We both had our own ideas about things and were always squabbling, but that didn't mean I didn't think a lot of my brother. I did.

'Why don't you look in the paper,' Phil suggested. 'I saw a show jumper advertised in the Saturday rag,' he went on. 'Sounded all right and only a few hundred quid. Why don't you go and see it?'

I was furious with him. His only interest was the farm though I had to admit that he was a great help to Dad. But farming wasn't my line and Philip had no patience when I was practising with Shelly or helping at the stables. He thought it a complete waste of time.

'You know perfectly well,' I told him loftily, 'that if you want good stock you've got to pay for it. I've done really well so far and Bruce says I'm good. I just need more experience but I must have the right horses. It's like starting a business. You've got to invest money into it to begin with before you make any profit.'

'Fine chance of profit,' snorted Philip. 'It would take you years to make up that money. You should be able to see that,' and, shoving back his chair, he put on his gumboots and went into the yard.

'Don't be late for school,' Mum called after him. He had certain jobs to do before he left in the morning and it didn't seem to worry him if he was late. To his mind, schooling wasn't going to be much use to him if he was going to be a farmer.

'It's hopeless, then,' I said, dejectedly. 'I might as well settle for an office job and be done with it. As it is, I've nothing to ride next Saturday. I'll just have to go and watch.'

'Let's look at it this way,' said Dad. 'You haven't even got a job yet. Once you start work, I'll try and make you a loan, but I shall expect you to pay me back so much each month. And another thing, I would want to see any animal you propose to buy. I don't trust these horse dealers and I know something about horses myself.'

Then there *was* hope. Dear old Dad. He was always fair. I would go over to Studlands now and see Bruce about the chestnut colt. If I explained the situation to him and offered to put a down payment on the colt, I felt sure he would accept it. After that I'd go into town to the job centre and see if I could come up with something. Now Dad had made this offer, I didn't much mind what sort of a job it was, so long as I could save enough to pay him back.

I pushed back my chair and was about to follow Philip.

'There are a few things to be done here first,' Mum reminded me.

I pulled a face. 'When I get back, Mum. Please.'

'Now,' said my mother and, reluctantly, I went upstairs and tidied my room and then washed up the breakfast things, by which time forty precious minutes had gone by. Life at home had its drawbacks, but on the whole we all got on well together and it was the only way I could keep horses and train them.

I walked over to the barn. Bess, the collie, got up to greet me, wagging her tail. I got out my bike and rode over to Studlands, thinking of the chestnut colt which would soon be mine.

Bruce Langford was leaning over the rails of the ring, watching the youngsters being schooled. He was a tall, good-looking fellow in his late twenties with sleek, black hair. He knew all there was to know about horses and had little patience with anyone who didn't measure up to his ideas of horsemanship. I'd heard that he didn't own the stables himself, but had gone into partnership with a wealthy stockbroker in London. I didn't know if that was true though.

I went and stood beside him and gazed at the colt which was being lunged on a long rein. The sun caught his chestnut coat and turned parts to gold. He was well formed with powerful muscles and held his head high. His ears were pricked and he looked about him, taking an interest in everything.

'He's beautiful,' I breathed.

Bruce turned to me with a grin. 'You want him for yourself, don't you?' he teased.

'Tell me how much you're asking for him and I'll try to raise it.'

'That colt's going to bring in a good deal more than you'll ever afford,' he said. 'He's got great potential and I'm not at all sure that I'm going to part with him. I want to see how he develops.'

I was disappointed, but I suppose I shouldn't have expected Bruce to let me have him just like that. I would just have to be patient. At least Bruce knew that I wanted him and hopefully he wouldn't part with him without giving me a chance to buy him.

'As a matter of fact I wanted to see you,' he went on, looking at me closely. The way Bruce looked at me always made me feel a little uncomfortable, as though he was sizing me up. 'Have you got a job yet?'

'Not yet. I was taking a bit of time off, but I must find something soon.'

'Len's leaving. He wants to go back to Ireland. I need another hand in the stables. Interested?'

'What does it entail?' I asked cautiously.

'A bit of everything. Usual stable jobs and some help in the office would be useful. You understand a computer, I suppose?'

I nodded. I'd done a course when I left school.

'I'm also looking for someone to train up for show jumping. You could fit the bill, Paula. With a bit more practice you could be very useful to us. Needless to say a fair salary goes with it. What do you say?'

It sounded too good to be true and all the while I would be gaining experience under Bruce's expert tuition. I couldn't have a better teacher. Just the same, I thought I'd better talk it over with Mum and Dad.

'I'll give you my answer tomorrow,' I said.

He looked a bit surprised. 'Waiting to see if something better turns up?' he asked, an edge of sarcasm to his voice.

'No. I'm grateful to you, Bruce. I'd like the job, but I want to talk it over with my parents.'

'Good girl,' he said. It annoyed me that he was inferring that I was a child and had to ask permission for everything I did. I changed the subject.

'Shelly's lame,' I said. 'I can't ride her on Saturday.'

'That's bad luck.' He was thoughtful for a moment, then he said, 'I'm thinking of entering Ranger for the Novice Stakes. It's his first competition and I don't want him pressed. He just needs experience. Suit you?'

What a chance! 'Oh yes! Thanks a lot, Bruce.'

'You'd better come over and do some work with him this week,' he said. 'You need to get used to one another.'

Back home, I found Dad in the yard talking to Matthew. They were looking at the old tractor. The thing was always going wrong. Matthew was twenty-four and worked on his father's farm further down the valley. The Fletchers were popular farmers and prosperous, too. Matthew ran the Young Farmers' Club and he often came round to lend a hand when Dad was in difficulties. He looked up and smiled as I cycled into the yard.

'What's wrong this time?' I asked.

'The clutch again,' said Dad.

'Old age,' said Matthew with a grin. 'You really need to upgrade a bit, Mr Marshall.' He wiped his hands on his dungarees. 'I came across a small Fordson the other day that would just about suit you. Do all you would want around here. Good buy it was. Like to come along and see it?'

'Not at the moment, Matthew,' said Dad. 'This has got to last till next year. Even if I sell it, I can't lay my hands on a couple of thousand just at present.'

'I think we might help out there,' said Matthew. 'My father and I were talking and it would be a real pity to let this machine go. If you could see your way to letting us graze some of our young heifers on those water meadows of yours, it would help us out a lot. They'd be no trouble to you and someone would come over every day to keep an eye on them. If you're not using those meadows at present, we could perhaps do some sort of deal.'

Dad said that he would be welcome to graze the heifers on the water meadows, but he wanted to think about the tractor.

I wheeled my bike into the barn as Dad and Matthew continued their conversation and fixed up the details. Once again Matthew was helping us out and in such a way that it sounded as though he was asking Dad a favour, rather than the other way round. But I felt a bit uncomfortable. If Dad was that hard up, maybe I had been wrong in pressing him for the money for the colt.

I pushed the feeling away. After all, I had my career to consider. Dad had managed up to now and things would no doubt improve. They always did after a bad patch. We would never be well off like the Fletchers, but neither would we have to sell the farm, and soon Philip would be leaving school and could help Dad.

When I came out of the barn, Dad had gone indoors. Matthew was collecting his tools and putting them into a bag.

'Everything all right?' he asked. We had known each other for years and he knew all about my passion for horses. He used to ride a bit himself, but he never had time these days.

'Shelly's gone lame and I can't ride her next Saturday,' I told him. 'But I've just seen Bruce Langford and he's letting me ride one of his.'

'It's not the same as having your own though, is it?' said Matthew with some sympathy.

'No. I really need another horse at this stage.'

'And horses cost money and your dad isn't in a position to help much at the moment?' His eyes rested on me, brown and serious. He wasn't exactly good-looking but he had a nice open face and thick brown hair. He had the strength of an ox, too. I had seen him shifting bags of grain as though they were stuffed with feathers. I found myself hoping that Dad hadn't told him of my request for money. I had a feeling that Matthew would have disapproved.

'Your dad was saying you're still looking for a job?' Matthew said.

'Not any longer. Bruce offered me one this morning at the stables. It's something I'll really enjoy.'

Matthew was silent for a moment, then he said. 'That's great. You'll be close enough to lend your dad a hand from time to time.'

I felt another pang of guilt. I had rather neglected that part of things. Since leaving college and with the show season coming up, I had largely concentrated on training Shelly.

'I'm afraid I haven't been much help to him lately,' I admitted. 'Philip helps him a lot. He loves it.'

'It would be a shame if your dad had to get rid of the farm,' said Matthew. 'How long has it been in the family? Three generations now?'

'Yes,' I said, feeling rather miserable.

'I wish we owned our farm. As tenant farmers, we can never be turned out, providing we farm it well, but it's never quite the same as your own land.'

I knew how he felt. I knew every nook and cranny of this place, the copse bounding the north side where we used to play hide-and-seek as kids, the lane that ran down to the old mill workers' cottages and, on the south, the land stretching towards the water meadows. Years ago Philip and I used to take our friends to swim in the river. I couldn't bear it to fall into someone else's hands. One day I wanted to see my own horses grazing in those meadows and white railings lining the drive. There would be room for both Philip and me to do our own thing.

'Dreaming again?' Matthew teased. 'I'll bet it's about horses.'

I laughed. 'Right.'

He picked up his bag of tools and threw them into the back of the van. 'We're having a barbecue over at the farm sometime next month. Like to come?'

'Yes, please,' I said. He often invited me to a Young Farmers' function and I always went over at Harvest Festival for the service and supper in the barn, followed by country dancing. It was packed with young people but their talk was always about farming and my heart was with horses.

'I'll give you a ring, then.' With a wave he was off and I watched the van disappear round the corner of the buildings, and the dust of the hot dry summer rise as it sped down the drive.

Matthew was a good friend but quite different from Bruce who was offering me a great opportunity to make a future for myself in the show ring.

~2~

Strangely enough, my parents weren't too happy about my new job.

'You could be wasting your training, Paula,' Dad said.

'I'll be using a computer there. That's something that Bruce wants me to do.'

'Only occasionally though. Things change so quickly these days, you need to keep your hand in. Apart from that, Bruce Langford is not a man I like.'

'Why not? He's always been helpful to me. What don't you like about him?'

'Nothing specific,' said Dad, vaguely. 'I've heard that some of his deals aren't all that straight, but that may be rumour.'

It wasn't often I heard Dad criticise anyone. He was much more likely to stick up for them, so I was surprised. Just the same, I had already made up my mind to accept the job even if it had to be without Dad's approval.

'It's the job I want and I think I'm lucky to have the opportunity.'

'It seems as though you've already decided,' said Dad. 'I believe you've got your head screwed on right and there's some sense in it, so you should be able to cope.' That's as far as he would go but I was relieved that he wasn't going to try and make me change my mind.

When Saturday came round I arrived at the stables in good time. The horses had to be prepared for the show and loaded into the horse-box. We had difficulty with Ranger who, in spite of many previous introductions, still hated the vehicle and it took ages to get him on board.

When eventually we got started, I sat between Bruce and Len. The horses seemed to have settled down and Bruce drove carefully so that no undue swaying would upset them more than necessary. We arrived at the show above twelve and Bruce found a shady place to park. We unloaded the horses and they were given a drink and walked round to get used to the surroundings.

Ranger was fretful. He hadn't travelled well and his coat was dark with sweat, but Bruce's horse, The Flier, an older and more experienced animal, had a calming effect on him, just so long as he was close by.

My event for Novices was at two o'clock and I was already dressed in the uniform of the show ring, light breeches, shirt, and stock tied neatly round my neck. My black jacket hung in the back of the box along with my cap. I had pinned my long fair hair back so that it was out of the way. Bruce was a stickler for neatness.

After we had eaten our sandwiches, Bruce saddled up Ranger and I put on my number and mounted. I'd taken him over the jumps at the stables and once he settled down he was a fantastic jumper. Bruce had high hopes for him, but at the moment he was dancing about all over the place. I didn't think I'd be able to do anything with him.

'Walk him round a bit,' advised Bruce. 'Let him see what's going on and get used to the scene. He'll soon quieten down.'

I moved off, and everywhere were cars, horse-boxes and people. Music blared from the loudspeakers and this was interrupted by a running commentary on the events. It was ages before Ranger quietened down and I had his attention. I took him back to Bruce and he said I'd done well.

Another announcement came over the loudspeaker. 'That's your call,' Bruce said. 'Just relax and concentrate on getting him round safely. Good luck.'

I rode him into the collecting ring. We were sixth to jump and I watched anxiously as the first competitors did the round. My heart was hammering against my ribs and I felt sure I was transferring some of my nervousness to the horse. So far there had been only one clear round. Now it was my turn.

We trotted into the ring and I put him at the first jump, a simple row of railings, which he sailed over. He was steady now and I could feel his powerful muscles propelling him forward as he took off. He was doing very well. Then came the water jump and I urged him forward to give him enough momentum to clear the water. Safely over and now a combination of jumps. He got his stride right for the double fence and then we were faced with the wall. It seemed massive and was certainly higher than anything we had attempted at home.

He took off too soon and clipped off a block with his

hind leg and that upset him for the triple bar. I steadied him but he rapped it and I heard it fall behind us.

Bitterly disappointed, I trotted out of the ring, making my way to the horse-box where Bruce joined me.

'Not bad,' was his comment. 'You had him nicely under control and he did all that I expected of him.'

We stood with the horses under some trees, while Bruce waited his turn to go into the ring. The open event was an hour later and Len had gone off to take a look at the exhibitions.

I stood staring across the field, wishing I had qualified for the jump off. I could have done so much better, but I guess every competitor who enters the ring feels that way.

'Come on, cheer up,' Bruce said, smiling at me. 'You did better than I expected. If you stick at this, Paula, I reckon one day you'll be one of the front runners, but you've got to give it all you've got. It means absolute dedication. I think you've got it. You've got something else, too, that a lot of riders lack, something that makes the horses trust you. If a horse trusts you, he'll do anything for you.'

That, from Bruce, was praise indeed. I determined then and there that I wouldn't let him down. I'd make those words come true, no matter what.

An hour later, Bruce rode The Flier into the ring and completed a clear round. There were four others for the jump off and he went on to win the cup and a substantial cash prize.

As soon as the presentation was over, we loaded up and Len took over the driving.

'Ever had any driving lessons?' asked Bruce, on the way home.

'Not really. Only along the drive at home.'

'Then I think we'd better get you started. I'll need someone to help when Len's gone. Though,' he added with a grin in Len's direction, 'I reckon it won't be long before he's back. Eh, Len?'

'Once home in Ireland, it's for good,' said Len.

'Then we'd better get cracking. You can have a go with the old van round the field sometime. Get the feel of the gears and then I'll organise some lessons for you.'

'What about paying?' I couldn't ask Dad for any more at the moment.

'We need a driver, so the stables will pay.'

It was six o'clock before I got back home. To my surprise, there was a truck full of heifers standing in the yard and Matthew was there talking to Dad.

'Just in time,' said Dad, when he saw me. 'We were wondering how we were going to drive these beasts down the lane to the water meadows without losing any. Phil's got extra work at school today.'

I was none too pleased. I was tired and all I wanted was to get to my room and dream about the day and what Bruce had said to me. The last thing I wanted was to drive cattle across the countryside.

'Got something else on?' asked Matthew, noticing my hesitation.

'No,' I said. 'I just want to get out of these things.'

I went off to my room and changed into jeans and a shirt and took my time about it. When I got back to the yard the truck had gone, so I got on my bike and rode off to where I knew they would be. Matthew was already unloading the cattle and Dad wasn't anywhere in sight.

'It's OK,' said Matthew. 'Old Harry came round and he and your dad have gone on down the lane to prevent them going off in the wrong direction.'

'I said I'd come.' I felt put out that they hadn't bothered to wait for me.

'You can help me anyway,' said Matthew cheerfully. 'Stand over there. We don't want them turning back onto the road.'

I stood in front of the truck as they spilled out into the lane and we started to drive them down towards the river.

'Went to the show, did you?' asked Matthew when they had settled down. 'How did Shelly do?'

'I told you, I didn't take her. She's lame. I rode one of the horses from the stables.' It was useless telling him anything. Unless it concerned farming, he just didn't listen.

'Went all right, did it?' asked Matthew, turning back a young heifer that was trying to scramble up the bank.

'I didn't win,' I said.

'That's bad luck. Better with your own horse, perhaps.'

I wanted to talk about it, tell him what Bruce had said about my riding, but it was pointless. He didn't even seem to notice that I was dead tired. I thought once again how single-minded farmers are. I didn't see at the time that people who are involved with horses are just the same.

It wasn't until after we'd said Grace at supper that evening – Mum and Dad always insisted on it – that Dad asked how I'd got on.

'I didn't win, but Bruce was pleased,' I told him. 'As a matter of fact he said that I had a special feeling for horses and if I persevered, I would do really well one day.'

Silence. Then Mum said, 'That's great, dear, but I expect there's a lot of competition and you need to be quite well-off to buy the sort of horses that will win the big competitions.'

'No hope for you, then,' said Phil, seeing an opportunity to needle me. 'You'd better settle for something less ambitious.'

'There *is* a chance,' I protested. 'I'm working at the stables now and Bruce has promised me some good horses to ride. He's going to teach me to drive, too.'

'All for nothing?' asked Philip, sarcasm giving an edge to his voice. 'I'll bet he wants something in return.'

'Look,' I said, 'just because you're happy spending your life knee deep in mud, mucking out pigs and cattle, you've no right to expect everyone else to feel the same way. I happen to find farming extremely boring and I don't want that sort of life myself, so shut up.'

'Paula, Philip!' protested Mum, 'if you want to carry on like that, will you go and talk it over in the yard, not at table when I've taken the trouble to cook you a nice meal that you're not even tasting. I'm ashamed of you.'

'Sorry, Mum.' We were both contrite.

'Your mother's right,' said Dad. 'I'm tired of your arguments. Will you never learn tolerance? Paula has a right to be pleased at what Bruce has said to her. She's obviously good and might possibly do quite well one day if she sticks at it. But you've got to be sure, Paula, it's what you really want out of life – that this obsession with horses isn't just a flash in the pan. And you, Philip, won't make much of a farmer unless you listen and learn from other people and understand how the rest of the world lives. It's a hard life and you must have faith in what you're doing if you're going to succeed.'

We all knew that Dad wasn't making money at farming, but no one doubted he was a wise man and generous to anyone who needed help. He was right, of course, but he needn't have worried because both Philip and I knew what we wanted to do with our lives.

~3~

I had been working at the stables for a month now and Bruce allowed me to take over the care of the chestnut colt, under his supervision, of course. I fed and groomed him and each day I took him into the ring to school him. Bruce watched carefully on these occasions, as he was training me as much as the colt.

'Keep him up to the rein,' he said, 'and don't let his mind wander. Good. You're getting the idea.'

The colt was not only intelligent, but very affectionate and he would come up to me when I went to the field to catch him. He was a lovely animal and I longed to own him. But I was worried because, as he developed, his value increased and soon he would be way beyond my reach.

I was earning a good wage and I had little to spend the money on, except for what I gave Mum each week for my keep. This was only fair. She worked hard and spent hardly anything on herself. So I would be able to save quite a lot and, with the loan that Dad had promised me, I would have enough to invest in the colt. Once again I spoke to Bruce about it.

He wouldn't commit himself. 'Why worry about it?' he said. 'You're working with him all the time, and he's as good as yours without having to pay anything for him. You can't ride him yet anyway. He's too young, but so long as you're working here, no one else is going to take care of him. Isn't that good enough?'

I looked on this as a sort of promise from Bruce. At least I could be sure that no one else would have the colt.

The days settled into a steady routine. We began work at seven and started by mucking out and grooming. Breakfast was taken in the big house with Bruce and Len, who had not yet left. There were usually a couple of pupils there who paid Bruce for the privilege of training under him. It was part of the British Horse Society's exam which would enable them to teach. I wasn't interested in this side of it. My future lay in the show ring and I was the one not only to ride the best horses, but to be paid for doing it.

After breakfast, we went into the field and caught up any horses which were needed that day. Schooling and exercising took up most of the morning and when this was done, Bruce and I went into the house and tackled the mail. Bruce dealt with it quickly and efficiently, such things as entries for shows, appointments for people to come and see the horses, and ordering food for the animals. I understood all this because I'd sometimes done it for Dad. Book-keeping was another department. Bruce did most of this himself and I never saw the accounts nor had any idea at what prices the animals changed hands.

One morning he was sorting out the mail, putting some aside to be answered and the rest into the wastepaper-basket.

'Listen to this one,' he said. 'I don't know what people think we are – a benevolent society or something. It's from a school in London for children with special needs, whatever that means. This Mrs James wants to find some stables where their kids can ride. Ah yes, she goes on about it here. The children have never ridden before but as it is so therapeutic for them, she is keen for them to start. She has, apparently, heard of our stables and wonders if we would be able to arrange something for them. She's right off the mark,' said Bruce, tossing the letter into the wastepaper-basket.

'But aren't you even going to reply to it?' I asked.

'Waste of time. She should have done a little research in the first place and she would have saved herself a stamp. This is a place to train horses for the show ring, not to give riding lessons to kids who've never been on the back of a horse.'

'I think you ought to reply, Bruce, if only to say that you don't do that sort of thing, and perhaps suggest someone who does.'

'That's up to her to find out, isn't it?' said Bruce. 'Now take this letter . . .'

He went through the mail, dictating half a dozen letters. It bothered me that he didn't even intend to answer that one and, just as he was leaving, I pleaded with him again.

'Couldn't we arrange something for those children? If I could find some people willing to lend their ponies, could we use the ring? I'm sure we could find someone to teach them. Perhaps the pupils would help? It would be a really nice thing to do.'

'Absolutely not,' said Bruce. 'We're not in that line of business. As it is, I've got more work than I can cope with now Len's leaving. Put it out of your mind. I'd be grateful if you could get through those letters in time for the afternoon post.'

He went out, slamming the front door behind him, and I heard his footsteps going in the direction of the stable yard. I went over to the wastepaper-basket and, picking up the letter, put it in my pocket. Then I sat down at the computer and started on the mail.

I told the family about the letter over supper that evening.

'Can you think of any stables that might be able to help them out?' I asked.

Dad shook his head. 'I can't. Something like that needs to be well supervised. They'd need a large staff with carefully selected ponies. There's a scheme called Riding for the Disabled, but I don't think there's anything like that in this area. How many children are they thinking about?'

'About six or eight. If we could find enough ponies,' I said, looking at Dad, 'we could have it here, couldn't we?'

'Something like that needs going into very carefully,' he said. 'You don't know what sort of problems those children have. If they are handicapped, they would find it very difficult even to sit on a pony, let alone balance. You could find yourself in a lot of trouble and you'd have to be quite sure, too, that you could rely on your helpers. I wish you'd think things through before you make these suggestions, Paula.'

I knew I was inclined to rush into things, but this idea seemed to be such a good one. 'I want to help those children,' I said. 'I know several people with ponies who might like to help. I'm sure, if I tried, I could muster up a few.'

'Dad's right,' said Philip, dismissing the idea. 'How could you be sure everyone would turn up and give their time? What day would you have it on anyway?'

'It would have to be a Sunday, I suppose. I'm working in the week and often shows are on a Saturday. You could help, Phil.'

'You must be joking! I've got better things to do with my Sundays.'

Dad smiled at me. 'It's a nice idea, Paula, and one that's obviously needed. But I don't think you should worry. They'll find some stables somewhere to help them.'

I let the matter drop. It seemed there were too many obstacles at the moment, most of them reasonable and I would have to go over them carefully. The important thing was to find a place where we could hold these sessions and I was sure Dad wouldn't mind it being here. Then we had to find some reliable ponies with owners who would be willing to turn up regularly. I was really excited about the idea. Those kids would benefit so much from an association with ponies. I remembered clearly how much my own pony had meant to me. I used to tell Brownie all my troubles when no one else understood. If I had to lay the idea aside for a while, I wasn't going to give up on it.

I looked at my watch. Bruce had promised he'd give me a driving lesson this evening. He said we'd take the van into the long meadow and I could practise there. I got on my bike and set off for the stables.

Bruce was waiting and he drove until we reached the field when I took over and he explained the gears to me. It was difficult to begin with because there was no rear window in the van but I soon got used to it. I was doing all right but it bothered me when he leant close to show me the indicators and lights, and the way he put his hand over mine when I had difficulty in getting into gear. Bruce was attractive, but his closeness was disturbing and I was relieved when the lesson was over.

I had intended to tell him that I had taken the letter because I wanted to do something about it, but in the end I let the opportunity pass. It would only upset him and unless something came of my idea there wasn't much point.

When we got back to the stables, he said, 'A few more practice runs and you'll be ready for some lessons. It won't take you long, Paula. You pick things up quickly. Like to come down to the pub for a drink?'

I'd never been to the local. Dad didn't encourage it and I didn't want to go now.

'Thanks, Bruce, but I've got some work to do at home.' A look of annoyance crossed his face. If Bruce suggested something, he didn't like to be turned down, but I had to make it clear that although I was happy working for him, that didn't include anything else.

When I got back, I went through the Yellow Pages and made some telephone calls. I tried four riding stables within a radius of twenty miles to ask if they had facilities for riding for the disabled. No one could help. It sounded as though they had already been approached as they told me I was the second person to ask that week. They said that they did not have the facilities for anything as specialised as this.

It wasn't until the following Sunday that I got my first sign of encouragement. Mum and Dad always went to church on Sundays and although Phil and I used to go to Sunday School, over the years we had drifted away, except perhaps for Christmas and Easter. Sometimes they suggested that we might like to go along, and although Phil never did, I occasionally joined them. I found the service boring and although I had to admit that people like Matthew and my friend, Jenny, who went regularly, were really nice people, I couldn't understand why they set so much store by it.

Anyway, on this particular Sunday, I decided to go along with Mum and Dad. After the service, when they were talking to some friends, I spotted Jenny. She and I often used to ride together, but we hadn't seen much of each other lately. I went over to talk to her. She was pretty with dark wavy hair and big brown eyes – rather serious perhaps, but she had always been a staunch friend right through school.

'Haven't seen you for ages. What are you doing now, Jenny?'

'Nothing at the moment. I had glandular fever and I can't throw it off. I was going to travel around on a Eurocard this summer, but Mum won't let me go until I'm fit. I get so bored at home and yet I don't really feel well enough to go off somewhere by myself.'

'That's bad luck. Have you still got your horse?'

'Yes. I don't use him much now. I shall get rid of him before I go to college. I've still got Joey, too. I can't bear to part with him. He's such a super pony.'

Things were beginning to stir in my mind.

'Jenny, I've got an idea. Are you free to come over this afternoon and I'll tell you about it.'

'Sounds interesting. About two?'

When she arrived I took her up to my room and put on one of my tapes. I liked a background of music even when my friends were round. I told her about my new job and the chance Bruce was giving me to ride his horses in the local shows.

'You always were good,' she said. 'And it always surprises me. You're smashing to look at and kind of delicate. I don't know how you manage those horses. But anyway I'm glad you've had this break.'

I went on to tell her about the letter and Bruce's reaction, though I explained to her why he couldn't do anything about it. 'I've rung round the local stables and no one seems able to help. It can't be easy otherwise they wouldn't come so far out of London. I'm wondering whether it would be possible to start something here.'

'I don't see why not,' said Jenny. 'That's if you can find enough ponies and the right sort of people to help.'

'Would you be interested in helping to set it up this summer before you go to college?'

Jenny was thoughtful. 'I'd want to know more about it first,' she said. 'Couldn't we talk to someone who does this sort of thing, even if it's not in this locality? I think we should find out just what it involves.'

'I've thought of that. But would you be willing to give up every other Sunday to it? It's no good unless we're prepared to do that. If something better turns up, we can't just put the kids off. We must be there.'

'Of course,' said Jenny. 'I'll let you know but I'll tell you this much. If, after learning more about it, I decide to do this with you, I'll stick to it. It will be my job for the summer.'

'Jenny, I wasn't thinking of it as a job. There won't be any money in it. It's something I want to do for them. The ponies will be lent and the helpers will be voluntary, unpaid.'

'Of course. I agree with that. I was just meaning that it would be my project till I have to leave for college. I suppose when that time comes you'll be able to find someone to take my place?'

'I expect I will.' We looked at each other and grinned. 'Do you really think we could do it?' I asked Jenny.

'We mustn't look too far ahead,' said Jenny cautiously. 'We haven't even begun yet.'

~4~

The following Sunday, Dad drove Jenny and me down to Sussex. One of the stables I'd rung had given me the address of a school who ran Riding for the Disabled classes and they said we would be welcome to watch. When we arrived, the children were already mounted and each pony was led round the ring by an adult. We introduced ourselves to Mrs Hughes who was in charge of the school.

'These children have been learning about six months,' she said. 'We start them off very slowly so that they get to know the ponies and how to look after them. They're encouraged to help with the cleaning out and the grooming and then we teach them how to put on the saddles and bridles. It takes them a long time to get the hang of it and of course, it's quite beyond some of them. But it's important and they learn a lot by being in close contact with the ponies.'

'What are the problems?' I asked.

'Have you had any experience with disabled children?' asked Mrs Hughes. I shook my head.

'A lot of these children have behaviour problems and they can be quite rough with small animals and pull them about. Ponies are big enough to withstand this and if they don't like it, they'll let you know. The children instinctively learn how to treat them and grow very fond of them. The ponies teach them things that they might resent being told by a grown-up.'

'So there's more to it than just riding?'

'Exactly,' said Mrs Hughes. 'A lot of them are dependent on other people for almost everything they do, so they find that riding gives them a measure of independence. They can move on the ponies' backs without help and they get a tremendous sense of achievement from this.'

'What about physical disabilities?' asked Jenny. 'What are the problems we have to be watching for?'

'There are many. Each child has its limitations and I advise you to make it clear to the teachers at the school that it will be *their* responsibility. You are simply providing the ponies and the help and cannot be expected to be responsible for that side of it. You need to have some good helpers to give a feeling of security to each rider, without fussing over them.

It was daunting. Nevertheless I was intrigued by the many ways it could help the children. I could see that we would need to be very careful in our selection of ponies and helpers and explain to them exactly what we had to do. It was a big responsibility.

'We don't even have a riding school,' I told Mrs Hughes. 'We're just a bunch of young volunteers. Is there anything to prevent us doing something like this?'

'Providing you make it perfectly clear what you can offer, it should be all right. I would imagine they would send someone with the children who understands the problems. I think you should insist on this. I would also suggest that you get in touch with Riding for the Disabled who would advise you and might even encourage you to join, though you would have to meet certain regulations for full membership.'

My mind was full of ideas as we drove home. I knew it was going to be far from easy and a lot of spadework would have to be done before we even started. Jenny wouldn't make any promises before she had discussed it with her parents, and Dad still had strong reservations.

'I think it's too much for you to undertake,' he said. 'You've got your job and I think you should concentrate on that. What's Bruce going to say about this? I think perhaps you should get his views on it.'

'We'll have a team, Dad. Once we get going, we can share the responsibility.'

'At the moment the team seems to consist of one volunteer and one doubtful. That won't get you far.'

I was getting fed up with all the opposition. I needed to talk to someone who would give me some encouragement, someone like Matthew. He was about the most unbiased person I knew and he was interested in social problems. I was sure he would see it my way. I rang him and he suggested that I should come over and talk about it.

He had just come back from the evening service and his parents were out. He invited me to share an omelette.

'Let's hear about this idea of yours, then,' he said.

I went ahead and told him everything and he listened without interruption. 'I know there are problems,' I finished, 'but there always are with anything that's worthwhile. I do want to help those children, Matthew. Don't you think it could be done?'

'I think it's a great idea, but have you the time to give to it?'

'I don't think it's going to be all that hard once we get it going. We shall have to try out the ponies with their owners and see that they are absolutely reliable. We'll tell the school that we've had no experience and that they must be responsible for the children. We're just offering the facilities. I've always been so lucky, Matthew. I've had my own ponies and everything I want. I'd just like those children to have a chance to get the same fun out of it.'

'Well,' said Matthew, 'what do you want me to do?'

'I just wanted to talk to you about it.'

Matthew smiled at me and we looked at each other for a moment. I liked him so much and I wouldn't ever want to hurt him. He was too nice a bloke for that.

'If you want something that badly, I reckon you'll go ahead with it,' he said. 'You always were determined.'

Just before I left, he said, 'By the way, I wish your father would accept that tractor. Do you think he'd be offended if I brought it over? That old one of his isn't really fit to drive.'

'I don't know,' I said. 'I think he feels he should still pay you something for it and he can't really afford it at the moment.'

'He's letting us have the grazing and that's worth a lot. Besides, it seems a pity to let this one go. It's a bargain.'

I wasn't sure about Dad's financial situation and I wondered if he was keeping aside that money he had promised to lend me for a horse, when he should have been getting this tractor. Perhaps I'd have a word with him about it.

The next day I took Dad's advice and spoke to Bruce. After all, the letter had been addressed to him and it was about time I told him I'd taken it. I waited until we were doing the mail.

'Bruce, you know that letter you had the other day from the school, the one who wanted riding lessons for their children?'

He looked at me sharply. 'Yes.'

'When you said there was nothing you could do for them, I took the letter because I was interested in it.'

'That letter was addressed to me,' he said. 'You'd no business taking it off the premises. Certainly not without my permission.'

'I wanted to reply to it myself.'

'Then I want to know what you said.' I was a bit scared because he really was very angry. 'I hope you didn't suggest setting up a riding school?' His voice was loaded with sarcasm.

'Not a riding school, but we're thinking of providing a few ponies and helpers for the children,' I said.

He put down the letters he was reading. 'I don't understand you,' he said. 'You're ambitious and I've given you this job with plenty of opportunities. I believe you've got a great future ahead of you and there aren't many I can say that about. Now you're thinking of exchanging all that for some whim you've thought up. If you're going to get anywhere in this game, you've got to be single-minded, to the exclusion of everything else. It's tough, but it's the only way.'

'But if I organise a few sessions for those children in

39

my own time and at our place, why shouldn't I? I promise you that it won't affect my work in any way. I'm just as keen as ever I was to do well and I'm grateful to you for offering me the job. You know that, Bruce.'

He relented a little. 'Then just remember to keep it that way. I'm not interested in charitable institutions. There's no room for that in my life and I think that if you're to do your job properly, you won't have time either. You have no idea of the work involved in something like that. It's not my business what you do in your time off, but if you go ahead with this, it seems inevitable that you won't be giving your whole mind and energy to what we're doing here. I'm just warning you, that's all. I don't want to hear any more about it.'

It was no good arguing. Everyone was against it. They were only too willing to point out the difficulties and the annoying part was that they were right a lot of the time. Even Matthew had warned me.

Perhaps, I thought, I should give up the idea. I didn't want to risk things going wrong because I went ahead against advice. I determined then to put it firmly out of my mind. But it wasn't that easy. It kept creeping back. I even prayed about it. I asked God to make it clear to me, one way or the other, what he thought I ought to do. Perhaps I didn't have enough faith because there was no direct answer, and I can't say I expected one.

Then two things happened to prove me wrong.

The following Thursday, I was cycling back from the stables when I saw two people riding down the road in front of me. One was a girl of about ten on a nice grey pony and she was with a woman on a big chestnut. They turned into a yard just ahead of me. I don't know why, but I found myself following them in.

'Excuse me,' I said, 'but have you been here long? I know this house was up for sale a short time ago.'

The woman smiled. She looked nice and seemed pleased that I had spoken to them. 'Only a month,' she said. 'My husband is working in London and we have just moved down from the Midlands, horses and all. We just couldn't leave them behind. That's why we bought this place with plenty of room.'

'Then I'm pleased you've come,' I said. 'I have a horse of my own and I work at Studland stables in the next village. My name is Paula Marshall and we live at River Farm.'

'Nice to meet you, Paula. I'm Sally Owen and this is Deborah. Thanks for making yourself known to us. I hope we'll soon get to know you better.'

I didn't say any more. I got on my bike and rode off home, but I had a feeling that it wouldn't be long before I would be getting in touch with these people again.

Then, in the evening, Jenny rang.

'I've been thinking, Paula,' she said. 'Count me in on this riding scheme. I think it's a great idea. Count Brownie in, too. It's ages since he's done some useful work and he's so good with nervous children.'

'That's great, Jenny. It's the first positive response I've had so far, and it could be an answer to prayer. I was really beginning to get a bit despondent. Now we can go ahead and see who else would be willing to come in on the plan.'

'I was talking to a friend of mine the other day,' Jenny said, 'and she's interested. She's got an old pony, a bit slow but it's gentle and good with children. I think anyone who is willing to lend their ponies will want to help so that they can keep an eye on them and see that they don't get pulled about.'

'Fair enough. I think we should have a meeting,' I said. 'The other day I met a woman called Mrs Owen who has just come to live in the village. She was riding with her daughter. Shall I ask her if she's interested? It could be very valuable to have an older person. What do you think?'

'Great. You get to work on her and I'll try and think of some others.'

The meeting was held in our dining room on Saturday evening. Dad was there. He said it was his field we were going to use and he wanted to know what was going on, but he insisted that I should do the talking.

Philip decided to come. I told him if it was just out of curiosity, he wasn't wanted. He'd have to contribute something. He asked how he could do that till he knew what it was about. Jenny came with her friend and, to my delight, Mrs Owen said that she was interested. The amazing thing was that she had once taught in a riding school where they used to have a class for disabled children.

We spent ages going over it but we were unanimous in wanting to give it a try. It was decided that we should write a letter to the school, offering them a place to ride, with ponies and helpers for six children. We explained that we were not a riding school, but a group of young people who were willing to lend their ponies and help the children. We stressed that we had no experience in teaching and we would expect the school to be responsible for the children. We suggested the first ride could be held in a month's time and there would be no charge.

A letter came by return saying that two people from

the school would come down and talk to us about it. Word soon got around about what we were doing and offers of help began to come in. We tried out all the ponies. They had to be quiet, sure-footed with nice temperaments and utterly reliable. Some of them proved unsuitable, but we were careful to encourage everyone who had offered help and invited them to come along to the first session.

Now things were really taking shape and the only worry I had was that Bruce was so much against it.

In spite of my enthusiasm for the children, I was still deeply involved with Studlands. I wanted to prove to Bruce that it would make no difference to my work at the stables. I was every bit as keen on my job and, of course, on my career. If anything, I arrived for work earlier than usual and never left before five. Bruce was very pleased with the progress we were making with the chestnut colt and congratulated me on it. I thought it was a good moment to bring up the subject again.

'Bruce, I wanted you to know that we've decided to go ahead with the riding scheme I was telling you about.' His face darkened and I rushed on. 'There's a lot of support from local people and they have offered their ponies and their help. I think it will be quite easy to run, once we get it organised.' I thought the fact that there were plenty of people involved might convince him that I wasn't going it alone, but I knew from his expression that he felt just as strongly about it.

He was silent for a moment, then he said, 'I think you're making a big mistake. You're wasting your time. Perhaps you'd be better off running a riding school. One thing's certain, the two won't mix.'

~5~

Bruce had a hot temper but it had to be said that, having spoken his mind, he didn't dwell on a disagreement. The riding project was not mentioned again and I was determined that he would have no cause for complaint about my work. Neither had I any intention of giving up on it now we had so much support.

Our first meeting took place on the last Sunday in June. It was a bright, sunny day and we were all there with the ponies groomed and the tack cleaned. The amazing thing was that Philip turned up. He had already helped to prepare the paddock and found mounting blocks for the children, but I hadn't expected him to take part in the lesson. Not only was it useful to have him there, but he seemed to enjoy it.

Mrs Owen had somehow managed to find some hats for the children and, as we stood waiting, a small bus drove into the yard and a red-headed fellow of about thirty jumped out and introduced himself as Don. He was followed by a woman who had been down before when two of the teachers had come to discuss the project with us.

They opened the back of the bus and slowly the children emerged. There were six of them, varying in ages and sizes. Some of them seemed to have difficulty in controlling their movements and one of the older girls had strange facial expressions, and a speech impediment. Don and the teacher, Jean, spoke to them slowly and explained that they must listen carefully and do what we told them.

They were dressed in jeans with a variety of footwear and, having sorted out the hat sizes, we introduced the children to the ponies, explaining how they liked to be treated. Then we gave them some carrots to feed to them. While they were doing this, Don and Jean told us a little about each child and their limitations. Don explained that he was a policeman and said he drove the school bus in his spare time.

'It's always useful to have a driver and I love these kids,' he said. 'I've got one of them myself, but she's not old enough yet to come along. Mary, that's my wife, is at home now looking after her.'

It wasn't until the second half of the lesson that we allowed the children to get on the ponies. They stood quietly while we adjusted the stirrups and told them how to hold the reins.

My charge was a little boy called Billy. He was smaller than the others and he was lame, but he seemed to have no fear. I let him sit on Brigand's back for a while to get the feel of it and then we moved off slowly with one of the helpers walking beside the pony. Once when I glanced at Billy I got my first thrill of pleasure when I saw the expression of sheer rapture on his face. If it meant this much to just one of these children, then it was well worth doing.

Don suggested that as this was the first time they had ridden they would tire quickly, so we helped them to dismount and they were quite happy stroking the ponies and talking to them. The hour soon passed and then Don told them it was time to get back onto the bus. Before they left, we arranged the next meeting and then waved them good-bye. It was good to see their happy little faces at the window waving back.

'Well,' said Mrs Owen, 'I think we can say that it was successful.' We all agreed on that, but we decided to have a meeting the very next evening to go over the lesson and talk about any problems that might arise. Mrs Owen was very encouraging, but she warned us that we mustn't go ahead too quickly. The important thing at the moment was to let the children enjoy the ponies and gain confidence.

The trip to the riding school had in no way prepared us for coping with the children. I don't think any of us had any idea of the effect their disabilities would have on us. For me, anyway, it was the first time I had come into close contact with something like this, and I was shocked at how much concentration and effort had to be put into the simplest of movements. I felt angry too. It was so unfair that some children had to go all through life like this, seeing everyone else having a good time.

A few days later I came back from work and found Matthew and Phil putting up posts in the paddock. Matthew looked up when he saw me and grinned.

'Philip and I have decided that you need some sort of

a ring here. It's safer than leading the ponies in an open field where something could upset them.'

'I was thinking that myself, Matthew, but it's going to cost an awful lot, isn't it?'

'It's my contribution,' said Matthew. 'I can get the timber cheaply and if Phil will give me a hand, it won't take long. Later on I might have a go at patching up that old shelter. You'll need somewhere to put the children if it comes on to rain.'

'I think it's very nice of you both,' I said enthusiastically.

Phil wandered off. He'd finished his job and now I'd arrived, he wasn't going to hang around.

'We might get a load or two of sand,' Matthew went on. 'If it rains the ground could get a bit slippery.'

'I wish you could have seen the children,' I said to him. 'They got so much enjoyment out of it. But you've no idea, Matthew, how handicapped some of them are. I think it's awful that some kids are born like that. Don was telling me that a lot of them have behaviour problems as well which makes it difficult to help them. Do you think they have to put up with teasing from the other kids, too?'

'Not as much as you'd think,' said Matthew, measuring the distance between two posts. 'Children are often more understanding than adults and a good deal kinder.'

'It's so unfair though. God can't want children to be like that. Why does he allow it?'

Matthew straightened up and looked at me. 'We blame God for so many things, don't we? You're right, though. He doesn't want people to be sick or disabled, but for one reason or another, a lot of people are. Some have tragic lives while others seem to get it all their own way. We're not a race of perfect humans, living in ideal conditions. God's given us free choice and sometimes we choose badly and innocent people suffer because of our selfishness. We can't see the whole picture as God does and we tend to judge him by our own limited understanding. When we don't think he's managing things the right way, we blame him.'

'So you think the troubles of the world are our fault? Nothing to do with God?'

'I think they have a lot to do with God, but that's because he wants to be involved with them. He might not change them, but he wants to help us through them. Perhaps we should try and see it like this – there are plenty of tragedies and what you call unfairness in the world, but I think that God uses us to try and make things better for the ones who aren't so fortunate as ourselves.' Matthew picked up the hammer and asked me to hold a bit of wood steady. Then he said, 'Seems to me that's what you and your helpers are doing for these kids.'

I was cheered by this. I was glad we were doing what we could, but it wasn't exactly the point I was trying to make.

'Just the same, I think I'd feel resentful. Don't you think they do?'

'No,' said Matthew. 'Did that strike you? I have an idea that sometimes people with disabilities have a closer relationship with God, simply because they're up against it and they know they're dependent on him. Most of us feel that we can manage very well without him and hardly give him a thought. God loves us and wants to have a personal relationship with each one of us, but he can only do this if we ask him.'

'What about the people who don't know about God?'

'I think in some cases he makes himself known to them, perhaps when they're in trouble and looking for spiritual help. It also puts a responsibility on us, don't you think, to tell as many people as we can about him?'

'I don't believe in going about Bible punching,' I said. 'I'd have no idea how to set about it.'

'There are plenty of other ways we can show God's love to folk,' said Matthew. 'We don't always have to talk about him, not until we're asked, anyway. But we can give a helping hand here and there or offer sympathy when someone's in trouble. If we're trying to live the sort of life God intends us to, I reckon folk notice and start asking questions.'

Matthew never talked a lot, not unless he felt deeply about something and then he'd go into it at length. He was the sort of person who listened and noticed things, quietly in his own way, the way that country folk often have.

'When did you become a Christian?' I asked him.

'When I was about twelve,' he said.

'Was it a dramatic moment, or did it gradually happen?' I was curious.

'We had a very good teacher at school and he had a lot to do with it. I suppose it was gradual, but when I made my commitment, I was absolutely sure about it. That's the way it happened to me but then, everyone comes to it in a different way.'

'How do you know when you're a Christian? I was confirmed, but it didn't mean all that much at the time. I don't think I could call myself one now.'

'You'll know all right. When we understand how much God loves us, we want to know him better and we want to do things his way.'

'Does it really make so much difference?' I asked him. 'Surely life goes on much the same?'

He shook his head. 'It's not the same at all. Claiming to be a Christian means changing our attitudes and actions. There are no half measures. It means total commitment to God and it influences every aspect of our lives.'

'It might sound selfish, Matthew,' I persisted, 'but what do you get out of it? You offer your life and your independence to God, and what do you get in exchange?'

'Everything. Freedom from fear, strength when things get tough, guidance when we have to make decisions. We have a sense of purpose and, for those who belong to him, the promise that one day we'll be with him.'

That was beyond my comprehension, but I wanted to know more. 'This commitment you were talking about, Matthew, what does it mean?'

'As soon as we commit our lives to God, he wants to change us. It's rather like a gardener. He cuts out the rotten wood, so to speak, and gets some good strong shoots coming up. He wants us to become more like Jesus and we have to turn to the Bible to find out about that. You see, however much we try to live decent lives, it's not enough. He wants total love and obedience. Once we've agreed to that, the results can be amazing. It doesn't mean that we're not going to suffer or face tragedy. More likely than not, we will, but he's there to give us strength and courage.'

I was silent. I felt far removed from what he was saying. It might be easy for Matthew to believe, but I didn't think I could. Besides there was another thing. If I always had to be worrying about what God wanted me to do, I would lose my independence and, at the moment, I didn't want to do that.

Matthew was looking at me, waiting for me to say something and when I didn't, he turned his attention to a board he was nailing into place.

'Could you hold it firm?' he asked. 'Don't let it slip again.' I adjusted the plank and supported it while Matthew selected a nail and drove it in.

'There,' he said, throwing his tools into his bag. 'That's enough for now. I need more wood and I'll finish it off tomorrow. I'm going down to the river now to have a look at those heifers. Fancy a stroll?'

He fell into step beside me and we crossed the paddock and climbed over the stile into the next meadow which dipped steeply at the far end towards the river. Here we stopped. The herd were gathered at the bottom under the shade of the trees, whisking away the flies with their tails.

'They're a good lot this year,' said Matthew, 'and I reckon they're all in calf. A water meadow is the best place for them in the summer.'

I was looking across the river towards the downs. The evening light cast a purple shadow across the slopes in sharp contrast to the brilliant yellow of the fields of rape in the foreground. It was one of my favourite views and at this time of day, it was at its best.

'Glorious, isn't it?' said Matthew, looking at me, his brown eyes warm with pleasure. 'Must be one of the best views in the country. I reckon we're pretty fortunate living in a place like this while all those poor folk have to sit in trains and traffic jams before they start work.'

I wouldn't want to live anywhere else. Not only did I love this place, but I had a super job with all the opportunities I needed. 'It's just as well we don't all like doing the same thing,' I said, 'otherwise we'd have the town people commuting to the country to work each day.'

'No way,' said Matthew. 'It's in your blood. You've got to be brought up to it. It's a hard life when all's said and done and not everyone could stand it.' His attention was on the cattle. 'Wait here a moment. I just want to take a closer look at those animals.'

He ran down the slope while I sat down on the bank to wait. A close watch has to be kept on each animal in case something is amiss. Unless it's spotted at an early stage, it could spell trouble and might mean the ultimate loss of an animal.

When he came back, he took my hand to help me up and held on to it as we walked back together.

'Are you going to carry on working for Bruce? Seems a pity when you've got this farm. Perhaps one day you can set up on your own.'

'I'd like to,' I told him. 'But I can't afford the horses at the moment. I'd never be able to compete against Bruce, anyway.'

'I saw him in the pub the other evening,' said Matthew. 'He was talking about you.'

'What did he say?'

Matthew hesitated, then said vaguely, 'He seems to think you've got a lot of talent.'

'He doesn't like the idea of the children coming to ride.'

'I gathered that. He thought you were wasting your time. You should know by now where your priorities lay, he said. A bit unfair, I thought, and I told him so.'

I shrugged. 'I don't care,' I said. 'He can think what he likes but I intend to go on with it.'

But it did bother me. It was one thing telling me he disapproved of the school, but quite another to discuss me with other people, as though he had some claim on me.

~6~

A few days later I was in Ranger's box, grooming him. His coat was really sleek now and he was doing fine. He had quietened down and, as I rode him regularly, I was getting used to his little quirks, the habit he had of veering off to the left of a jump and the way he sometimes took off too soon. But he leapt like a deer and Bruce expected him to do well at the Midland show in a few weeks time.

We had about a dozen horses at the stables. Bruce did a lot of buying and selling and there were constant changes. He also had horses at livery which he trained for the owners who didn't want the hassle. I believe the prices he charged for this were exorbitant.

There was a fellow coming over from Ireland to take Len's place and meanwhile old Sam was helping out. He used to work for Bruce but he didn't ride these days. Some of the horses could be ill-tempered and the men often shouted at them and gave them a clout. My approach was different. I talked to them quietly, caressing them, and they responded to this. It was my belief too, that horses often perform better for women; with a few exceptions, of course, but girls are gentler in their ways.

I had just put Ranger's saddle on when, to my surprise, I saw Bruce leading the chestnut colt into the ring. With him was a man I had not seen before. Bruce walked him round while the stranger leant on the railings watching the colt being put through his paces. It was usually my job and at first I couldn't understand why Bruce hadn't asked me to do this. He'd said nothing about it though, and soon the reason became painfully obvious. He was thinking of selling the colt.

When the man had gone, I went in search of Bruce.

'Who was that?' I asked.

'A fellow I know.'

'He wants to buy the colt?'

He looked at me with a rather supercilious smile on his face. 'That's right.'

'I thought you said you were going to keep him.'

'Since when do I have to ask your permission to sell a horse from these stables?'

'I'm not suggesting you ask me,' I retorted, 'but when I tried to discuss it with you, you said that you wanted to see how he turned out. You know how much I want him.' I was so angry I had forgotten I was talking to my boss.

'Sometimes an offer is made for a horse which far exceeds expectations and it would be foolish to turn it down.'

'Have you sold him then?'

'I'm thinking about it.'

'How much has he offered?' I had no right to ask these questions, but I was beyond caring.

'More than you could possibly afford, and nearly twice as much as he's worth at the present time, untried as he is. For that price, I can buy a really good animal and put it to use immediately. Come on,' said Bruce, putting his arm round my shoulders, 'it isn't the end of the world.' I shook off his arm and moved away.

I was miserable for the rest of the day. I loved that colt. I understood him and I, more than anyone, knew how to handle him. What sort of a home was he going to and would he be well treated? This wouldn't bother Bruce. Once he'd made a good sale, that was it. I felt now that I couldn't trust him, but I still depended on him to give me the opportunities I needed.

I went off early that evening. I couldn't bear to hang around any longer. When it came to supper, I picked at my food and Mum asked what was the matter.

'The chestnut colt's been sold,' I told them. 'Bruce let him go because he had a good offer for him.'

'That's part of the business,' said Dad, 'training up stock and selling it.'

'But he knew I wanted him. I offered to put a down payment on him and pay the rest off each month.'

'And where were you going to get that?' asked Philip, ever ready to ask embarrassing questions.

I looked across at Dad. 'Dad said that when I'd got a job, he'd lend me some, provided I paid it back.'

'That's right,' said Dad. 'Now it seems this colt you're talking about has been sold to someone else. But there'll be others. He was a bit on the young side for your purposes anyway, and I dare say Bruce might find you something else.'

No one seemed to understand how I felt about that horse and the dreams I'd built on him.

'I'd put so much work into him,' I told them. 'He'd do anything for me and I don't even know if he's going to a good home. Bruce didn't consult me. That's what's so unfair.'

'Where were you going to keep him?' asked Dad.

'At the stables, of course. He was being schooled there.'

'How much does it cost to keep a horse at livery and have him schooled?' Dad asked.

'I don't know, but it's very costly.'

Dad was spelling it out. 'So you were going to pay for his schooling or do it in Bruce's time? I presume he wouldn't be throwing all this into the price of the animal?'

I got the point. 'We could have come to some arrangement,' I said, off-hand.

'Did he ever promise the colt to you?' asked Dad.

'Not exactly, but he knew I wanted him. He could have given me a chance.'

'I also gather,' Dad went on, 'that Bruce wasn't too keen on this riding scheme you've set up?'

'No. He was against it. What's that got to do with it?'

'But you went ahead with it just the same. That's all right. You do it in your time and it doesn't affect your work, but it seems to me that he's under no obligation whatever to let you have this animal. Don't you agree?'

When I said nothing, he went on gently, 'Look, Paula, we'll find a horse for you to replace Shelly, but be patient. It has to be carefully chosen.'

I knew what a sacrifice Dad was making to do this, and he would never break a promise. I don't know what got into me, but instead of thanking him, I said, 'I don't want any other horse. I only wanted the chestnut colt.'

I pushed back my chair, ran up to my room, and burst into tears.

I went off to work early the next day. I felt at loggerheads with everyone. I didn't want to face Mum and Dad, nor did I want to see Bruce. Dad had been so good about letting us use the field for the riding and giving it his support that I felt pretty bad about my behaviour the night before.

As I went to the barn to get my bike, I saw his old tractor standing in the yard. It had a trailer attached so he must have been using it recently. I stood looking at it for a moment. It was just as important to him as the colt had been to me, more so probably, because our livelihood depended on it. I felt sure that he hadn't taken up Matthew's offer to upgrade it because he'd already put the money aside for me.

As it turned out, I didn't have to face Bruce that day. He'd gone off to see someone about a horse, so I went through my usual routine, putting the colt through his paces and working with Ranger for a while. Then I went into the house and looked through the mail. There wasn't anything that looked particularly urgent, so I put the letters in a neat pile on Bruce's desk.

When I got back home, I went to look for Dad. Mum said he was taking hay to the cattle. There hadn't been any rain for weeks and the ground was like brick with a covering of dried grass, useless for animal food. All this meant extra expense at a time of year when food should have been plentiful. But then all the farmers were in the same boat.

I found him cutting the string off the bales and forking

it about for the bullocks.

'Dad . . .' I began.

He looked up and gave me one of his nicest smiles. He never bore any resentment or, if he did, he didn't show it.

'Hullo, love. What brings you here?' I felt a stab of guilt. He would never have asked Philip that question. It wasn't often I turned up when there was work to be done. I wasn't that interested, but Philip spent all his free time on the farm because he loved it, and that gave Dad a lot of pleasure.

'Dad, I wanted to say sorry about last night. I've been thinking about it all day and I was very ungrateful when you offered me that loan. I really am sorry.'

He came and put his arm round me and gave me a hug.

'I know that colt meant a lot to you,' he said. 'You'd set your heart on him and when you found out that Bruce had other plans, of course it hurt. Just the same, we have to face the fact that he was under no obligation to let us have him. I'm afraid with things as they are at present, I couldn't stretch to any more, and it sounds to me as though he got a very good price for that animal.'

He was putting himself on my side, saying 'we' and that made me feel better. It meant that Dad wasn't against my ambitions, just that he couldn't afford to invest in them.

'Thanks, Dad. I know things are difficult at the moment.' I looked at the tractor. 'Couldn't you upgrade that old thing? You really do need to change it.'

'I'll think about it. It's kept going all these years. A few more months won't make much difference.'

After that I felt very much happier. The colt didn't

leave immediately. Bruce told me that the new owner was pleased with him and wanted to leave him at the stables for further training. Bruce gave me credit for this and said that I was building on the good reputation of the stables. I think he was beginning to realise that the riding project wasn't making any difference to my work because he spoke about it himself one day.

'I hear you had the children riding again recently.'

'Yes. It's going well but we have to go very slowly. It's the first time any of them have been on a pony and they tire so easily.'

'What's the point, Paula? You're never going to make riders of those kids. What good are you doing them?'

He really believed that this was all there was to it. He saw everything in terms of success, and that meant the show ring and winning prizes.

'It's not the point,' I said. 'They love it and they don't get much fun in their lives. That's why we do it.'

The telephone rang in the yard and he went into the house to answer it. He had already lost interest.

When he came out again, he said, 'This show in the Midlands next week. It's too far to do it all in one day. We'll have to start very early on Saturday and spend the night up there. I'm arranging stabling nearby for the horses and I've booked rooms for us at an adjoining hotel so that we can keep an eye on them. Quite a few of the riders who come from far afield will be doing the same thing and you'll be able to meet them. It's a great get together.'

This was the first he'd said anything about being away for the night and it sounded a wonderful opportunity to meet some of the riders I'd always admired. I was really excited, but I'd reckoned without Dad's reaction.

61

I waited till we'd finished supper that evening. Philip was upstairs doing his homework and Mum had gone into the kitchen.

'Bruce was telling me about the arrangements he's made for the Midland show,' I said. 'It's too far to get there and back in a day, so the horses will be stabled overnight and Bruce has booked rooms for us in a hotel nearby.'

Dad was silent for a moment, then he said, 'You're not going, Paula.'

I stared at him. 'What do you mean? You know I'm riding Ranger in the Open Novices.'

'I'm not having you spending the night in a hotel on your own.'

'I shan't be on my own. Bruce is fixing it up. He says a lot of the riders stay there.'

'I don't like the idea and you'll have to tell Bruce that I won't allow it.'

I had seldom seen Dad so emphatic. He was usually prepared to talk things over and reason with me, but not this time.

'But he's depending on me to ride. The show won't be over till late and how would I get home? Bruce says there'll be a party afterwards and I can meet the other riders.'

'You can take a taxi to the station after your event and come home by train.'

'It would take ages and be terribly expensive.'

'It doesn't matter. I'll pay for it.'

Dad was asking the impossible. How could I go to Bruce and tell him that my father wouldn't allow me to stay overnight? He would laugh at me and I had no good reason to give him.

'Look, Dad,' I pleaded. 'I *must* go. It's my job. Just give one good reason why you don't want me to stay.'

'For the very reasons you've just given me. There'll be a lot of drinking and Bruce will be much too busy to bother about you. The horse world is a tough one and I don't think you're old enough to be part of it. Not yet. In any case, Bruce made no mention of staying overnight when he asked you to ride this horse, did he? Now I don't want to hear any more about it.'

I was so angry, I was near to tears.

'It would be better to tell him that you just won't let me go at all,' I raged. 'You won't even let me ride.'

'That's not true. If you like, I'll go and talk to him myself.'

'No!' Goodness knows what Dad would say to him and Bruce would ridicule me for not being able to fight my own battles. 'I'll tell him,' I said.

Much though I hated it, I would have to practise a little deception. Bruce was depending on me, not only to ride Ranger, but to help him when the show was over and on the long drive back. He couldn't do it all himself. It was my job, but that didn't seem to be a good enough reason for Dad. I would just have to play it along and tell him at the last moment that I was going anyway and that I intended to stay the night.

~7~

Ten days before the show it began to rain. After weeks of scorching sun when the earth became brick hard, the rain now torrented down and rivers formed in the yard and along the road, as the water poured off the fields. Bruce was worried about the horses.

'If it doesn't dry out by Saturday, it's going to be dangerously slippery,' he said. 'You can damage valuable animals in these conditions.'

Dad, of course, was glad of the rain. At last a film of green appeared over the fields and the potatoes already looked healthier. He had tried this crop as an experiment this year and it had suffered from the drought.

Thankfully, he hadn't questioned me again about staying away overnight, and I had no intention of mentioning it until just before I left, but one morning as I was setting off to work, Mum suddenly said, 'Dad's up against it this summer, Paula. I think we ought all to be helping him as much as possible.'

'But I can't, Mum. I've got this job all day and I'm tired when I get back. Besides, there's the children's riding school and that takes time. I can't be expected to do more.'

'I wasn't talking about work, dear,' said Mum. 'I think we should try to encourage him, not oppose his wishes.'

I knew what she meant, but I wasn't going to argue with her. If we got started on that again, I might have to make a promise I wouldn't be able to keep. Once this show was over, I would make up for it. I would really try to cooperate at home and I could see nothing in the future which might cause further disagreement. But on this one issue I had to make a stand and I was sure I was right.

Then the evening before the show Phil came to find me.

'Going to this show, are you?' he asked.

'Yes, tomorrow.'

'Are you going to do what Dad wants and come home afterwards?'

I looked at him, wondering if I could trust him. Then I said, 'No, I'm staying. Bruce needs my help and he's depending on it.'

'Dad will be pretty upset, you know. I think he's right. You might find yourself in all sorts of trouble.'

'What do you know about it?' I demanded. 'Anyway I'm eighteen and quite capable of looking after myself.'

'OK,' he said. 'Please yourself. But Dad's right about a lot of things and it doesn't matter what age you are, if he feels so strongly about this, I think you should go along with him.'

'It's none of your business,' I told him. 'This is

between Dad and me and I shall tell him in my own good time.'

Philip shrugged. 'I'll say no more then, but take care.'

The fact that Phil had opposed me upset me more than the arguments with Mum and Dad. He was quite sensible and it shook me that he seemed so adamant about this and I couldn't understand why. I wasn't a kid any longer and I had no intention of doing anything I didn't want to do. But I was committed to ride Ranger, and Bruce was confident that we stood a very good chance at this show. It was the opportunity I had been waiting for and I wasn't going to let anything spoil it. But somehow now, the edge had gone off my excitement.

That evening Dad had gone round to see a neighbour and by the time I went to bed, he still hadn't returned. Perhaps it was just as well, I thought. I could always ring from the hotel and it would save an argument. But next morning I had a better idea. I wrote a note telling them I wouldn't be back till Sunday and giving the name of the hotel where we'd be staying. I left it on the kitchen table and then quietly let myself out of the back door. It was five am. Bruce wanted to leave by six, and there was still a lot of work to be done.

We brushed down the horses and loaded them without any trouble, together with all the equipment. Being early, there was little traffic on the roads and Bruce drove steadily, arriving in good time. We unloaded the horses and led them round for a while to settle them and get them used to the atmosphere. The older animal had travelled well, but Ranger was in a sweat. He hated the horse-box, but presently I could feel him relaxing and we allowed them a short drink, before eating our sandwiches.

My event was at two o'clock. There were sixteen entries and Ranger and I had a clear round together with six of the other competitors.

Bruce was quietly optimistic and I listened carefully while he told me how to handle the next round. The higher fences weren't usually a problem for Ranger. He'd jump anything, provided he was concentrating, but on this occasion, we were up against some good horses. In the second round two of them rapped a bar and one failed to clear the water. Then, to my relief, one of the horses I had feared, unexpectedly refused the wall, leaving two of us for the jump-off against the clock. This could be a problem as Ranger was strong and inclined to bolt the course and I had quite a job collecting him as we approached the jumps. But he was fantastic that day and did just what I asked him. We both had clear rounds but, by taking a few risks and cutting corners, I managed to clip off a few precious seconds and completed the course just a shade faster.

I shall never forget how thrilling the applause sounded as I did my lap of honour and Bruce's praise afterwards really made me feel great. He did well, too, coming second in his event. Together we had won a substantial amount in prize money and, of course, it increased the value of the horses.

Later on, we took the horses to some stables a few miles away where we bedded them down for the night and gave them a feed.

'I'll come out later to take a look at them,' said Bruce. 'The hotel's only a few minutes away.'

We checked in and went to our rooms for a bath and change. Bruce said a lot of the riders would be meeting in the bar that evening and that he'd see me downstairs about seven.

I was really tired and lay in the bath going over the events of the day. I wondered what Mum and Dad would be thinking now. In spite of my success, I was worried about their reaction to my letter. Perhaps it was rather a cowardly way of doing it, but when they heard how successful we'd been, I was sure they would realise that I'd done the right thing. It would have been awful if I'd had to go to the station now on my own and get a train back. And it would have meant leaving Bruce to do everything himself. Caring for your horse and seeing that it was comfortable after a hard day's work, was an important part of the job.

I dressed carefully, putting on my new summer dress that Mum had bought me some weeks before. It was a pretty blue with a low neck and flared skirt. Sitting down in front of the mirror, I brushed out my hair which I always pinned up neatly when I was riding, and carefully applied a little make-up. I felt pleased with the result which made me look older.

The bar was full when I came downstairs and I spotted Bruce talking to a couple. I made my way over to him and he gave me a dazzling smile and asked what I'd like to drink. I had decided on orange juice and when he went off to get it, his friends congratulated me on my prize and said how well I'd handled a difficult horse. Throughout the evening I had lots of compliments and Bruce introduced me to some of the big names in the business. Everyone was talking horses, discussing the course and future shows. I might have been the youngest there but I felt completely at home in this environment. It was a world that fascinated me and one in which I

69

wanted to make my mark and the sooner I got started the better.

People were drifting into dinner. Bruce had booked a table for the two of us and I was glad that we weren't sharing with anyone else. He seemed to know everyone here and had been surrounded in the bar, particularly by the ladies, so I had no chance to talk to him. Now I wanted him to myself so that I could hear what he thought about the show.

When the waiter handed us the menu, Bruce said, 'Don't hold back. Choose something you really like. We can afford to be extravagant today.'

As I chose, Bruce was looking through the wine list and asked if I preferred white or red. I'd no idea, as I rarely drank wine, so I asked him to order.

'You were really great today, Paula,' he said and, seeing the admiration in his eyes, I knew I had come up to his expectations. 'If we keep this up, you know, we'll be a great team. I've had a spot of luck, too,' he went on. 'I think I've found the right horse for our stables. She's a lovely mare, quite young and perhaps a little on the small side, but that's no problem. You're no weight yourself and if they accept my offer, she'll make a very good investment. We'll take a look at her tomorrow and see what you think.'

The fact that he was taking me into his confidence meant that he actually valued my opinion. He was certainly giving me all the opportunities I could have wished for.

He was in an expansive mood that evening. 'That colour suits you,' he said, looking at my dress and at the same time, refilling my glass with wine. 'Do you know

I don't think I've ever seen you in a dress before. More's the pity.'

The meal continued leisurely. Everything was delicious and I allowed Bruce to refill my glass several times. He could be very amusing and for some reason that evening, I found everything he said incredibly funny, but as time went on, I began to feel sleepy and looked at my watch. It was past eleven.

'Like to come with me to have a last look at the horses?' he suggested. 'I want to make sure they're all right.'

I was feeling a little dizzy but I thought I should make the effort and I followed him outside. I was wearing high heeled sandals and it made me rather unsteady. Bruce took my arm and helped me along. There were a few people about coming back from the stables. It was a lovely clear night and it was exciting to be walking along a country road with Bruce. When we got to the stables we found a couple of chaps in charge who questioned us. You couldn't leave all those valuable horses without someone to keep an eye on them. Ranger and The Flier had boxes side by side and they were both munching contentedly in their stalls. When we spoke to them, they swung round and put their heads out of the boxes.

'They're fine,' said Bruce. 'We can turn in with our minds at rest now. We'll start off about nine tomorrow. No need to start too early.'

I felt better after the fresh air and I didn't mind when Bruce slipped his arm round my waist on the way back. Then, as we came into the shadow of some trees, he stopped and, drawing me towards him, he tried to kiss me. I was so taken aback that it was a moment before I pushed him away.

'Come on, Paula. What's the harm in a kiss to seal our success today?'

I felt a bit silly making a fuss about it, but just the same, I didn't like it.

'I'm tired,' I said. 'I want to get to bed.'

He was sympathetic. 'A cup of coffee will put you right. Come up to my room and I'll make us one.'

I was frightened then. This was getting out of control and I wasn't sure how to handle it. I quickened my pace for the short distance back to the hotel and went ahead of him up the steps.

As I pushed open the swing doors, I saw Matthew standing there, and the expression on his face swept every other thought from my mind. His face was white and drawn and he looked exhausted.

'Paula, your father's had an accident. I've come to take you home.'

~8~

When I came downstairs a few minutes later, Matthew was talking to Bruce in Reception. He took my suitcase and said that he would tell me what had happened on the way home. As I followed him to the door, I glanced at Bruce.

'It's OK,' he said. 'You'd better go.' But he looked annoyed. Matthew took my bag and carried it out to the car.

'It was that old tractor,' he said, once we were on the road. 'He was driving it across the field, that one with the steep slope at the farther end. All that rain had made the ground slippery and it seemed that one of the tyres burst and the tractor skidded towards the slope, over-turning at the bottom. Normally the safety bar would have protected him, but he must have been thrown out at an awkward angle and his legs were pinned under the bar. Fortunately it happened within sight of the road and a motorist saw what happened and got help quickly.

73

Your father was taken straight to hospital. His leg's broken in two places and they're worried about his back.'

'But is he going to be all right?'

'They can't tell yet. He's in a lot of pain.'

'It's my fault,' I groaned.

'What do you mean by that?' asked Matthew.

'He didn't want me to stay here for the night and I took no notice of him.'

'That didn't cause the accident,' said Matthew, but his voice was brusque. 'It was a combination of a dangerous machine and weather conditions. It could have happened any time.'

'How did you know where to find me?'

'Philip rang to tell me what had happened and said you were away at a show and that you wouldn't be back till tomorrow. When I heard how serious it was, I thought you would want to come home so I came to get you.'

'Is Dad conscious?'

'Yes, but when I left and that was about six o'clock, he was heavily sedated. Your mother and Philip were both at the hospital with him.'

'Oh God,' I prayed silently, 'please let him be all right. Please don't let him die.'

'He must have been terribly upset by my note,' I said presently. Was it only this morning that I had written it and sneaked out of the house without saying goodbye?

'What note?' asked Matthew.

'I left a message to say that I wouldn't be back till tomorrow. I didn't want an argument with him, so I wrote a note.'

'You wanted to make quite sure he wouldn't try to stop you?'

74

'He'd tried to do that already. He didn't mind me riding in the competition, but he was against me staying away for the night.'

'And yet you were determined to do that?'

'It was too far to get back the same day and Bruce had booked in at that hotel to be near the horses. Dad wanted me to come back by train, but it would have been difficult and very expensive. Besides, Bruce needed my help with the horses.'

'He'll have to do without it now, won't he?' said Matthew.

He was driving fast on the south-bound carriage-way, and I could feel his cold disapproval. I was feeling very sick and soon I had to ask him to stop. He took the next exit and waited while I deposited my supper, including the wine, onto the verge. Then I got back into the car and we set off again in silence. I had never felt so miserable and ashamed in my life and because Matthew knew the whole sorry story, it made it so much worse.

Tears which I couldn't control, streamed down my face and there was a cold knot of fear inside me. Supposing Dad should die? I would never forgive myself. I kept going over all the disagreements we'd had lately, the time when I'd asked for money for a new horse, my determination to start the riding school for the kids and now my refusal to come home after the show. Whenever it was practical, Dad had given me his support but not on the last issue and it was all too clear why. I'd made a fool of myself by drinking too much and I'd been flattered by all the compliments which had come my way, particularly from Bruce. If Matthew hadn't turned up I could have found myself in a difficult situation tonight. Dad knew what he was talking about, but it was too late now to think about that. I knew what Matthew was thinking of me and I didn't like it a bit.

In an effort to break the unbearable silence, I said, 'Thank you for coming up to fetch me, Matthew.'

'I hope I didn't interrupt anything?'

Perhaps I deserved that insinuation, but he needn't have been so unkind. It wasn't like Matthew, but I guess he was feeling pretty upset as well.

'You know, had you asked me, I could have met you half-way and brought you home. Something could have been arranged, I'm sure.'

'I couldn't, Matthew. It's an awful long way. I couldn't possibly.'

'In the end it would have saved a lot of hassle. Never mind. It's too late now, but you might bear it in mind in future. Now, when we get back, do you want to go straight to the hospital or shall I take you home first?' he asked.

'Perhaps we'd better go home in case Mum's back. If she isn't, please could you take me to the hospital?'

'Yes. That's best.'

But when we reached the house, the lights were on and Matthew came in with me. Mum was pouring a cup of tea and looked up. I went straight to her and burst into tears and she put her arms round me and hugged me.

'How is he?' Matthew asked.

'He's sleeping now,' she said. 'They persuaded me to come home and get some rest. They promised to ring if there's any change. Philip's gone to bed, but I wanted to wait for you.' She was looking as white as a sheet and desperately tired.

'Then I'll get back,' said Matthew. 'I'll be over again

early tomorrow to have a look at the cattle, and we'll sort out how best to manage things here. Philip and I will get some sort of routine going between us.'

It hurt that he had cut me out of his calculations, but I suppose I deserved it.

'Try not to worry,' he said, 'he's strong and he'll pull through, but if there's anything I can do, don't hesitate to ring me, no matter what the time is.'

'We can't thank you enough,' said Mum, 'specially for bringing Paula back.'

He didn't answer. He was already outside.

'Sit down, dear,' said Mum. 'Let's have a cup of tea.'

'Mum, I feel so awful. It's all my fault, isn't it?'

'Nonsense, dear. Didn't Matthew tell you? It was a burst tyre. The tractor skidded.'

'I know, but don't you see? Matthew gave Dad the chance to change it. He warned it was dangerous, but Dad said it could wait. I'm sure it was because he was putting aside the money he'd promised me for a horse.'

'You mustn't think that. It was just that he hadn't made up his mind.'

'Was he very upset about the note?' I asked.

Mum was always practical and perhaps she saw how desperate I was. 'Look, dear, no good will come of us sitting here wondering who's to blame. It's no use saying that he wasn't upset. He was. You don't usually go against his wishes, not without good reason and he's never been one to ask you to do something unless it makes sense. He couldn't understand why you hadn't spoken to him yourself instead of writing that note. It wasn't like you. He was certainly worried about you, but that had nothing to do with the accident. They are two separate things.'

'I can't bear the thought of him lying there so ill, thinking about what I've done.'

'That's as may be,' said Mum, 'but it seems to me you're feeling pretty sorry for yourself at the moment. Now we'd best go to bed. We'll talk about it tomorrow.'

She gave me a hug and a kiss. I felt a bit better after that, but she hadn't let me off the hook and I would have to come to terms with it myself. Nevertheless, as soon as I got into bed, I fell into a deep sleep and didn't wake till nine the next morning with a terrible headache. I pulled on my jeans and went downstairs. Philip was already out, feeding the pigs.

'I'm sorry I overslept, Mum. Have you rung the hospital yet?'

'Yes. He's much the same. They'll know more after the doctors have been round. I'm going to see him as soon as you've had breakfast. You'll want to come?' she asked.

'Of course.'

'Philip came in and poured himself a cup of tea. He gave me a long look but he didn't say anything.

'We're going to see Dad,' said Mum. 'Are you coming with us?'

'I've work to do here first,' he said shortly. 'I'll go along later.'

When we arrived at the ward, Dad was lying in bed with his leg in traction. His face was lined and grey and he looked so much older. It was awful seeing him like that. I could never remember him being really ill before.

'Hullo,' he said when he saw me, 'I thought you were in Derbyshire.' His voice was weak and I had to lean forward to catch what he said.

'I came back, Dad. Matthew came and got me.'

'Went all that way, did he? How did you do?' His words were slurred and it must have cost him an effort to talk.

'All right,' I said. 'I won my event.'

'Well done.'

'And Bruce came second in the Open. It was a good day for us.'

'Made it worthwhile going, then?'

'Yes.' I smiled at him but I couldn't stop the tears. 'I'm sorry, Dad, about that note. I didn't know what else to do.'

He didn't say anything. I think he felt too ill to go into all that.

'Does it hurt terribly?' I asked him.

'Not so bad now. They gave me something to make me sleep. 'fraid I'll be out of action for a while, though.'

'You mustn't worry about that,' said Mum. 'Matthew's promised to keep an eye on things, and Philip can do quite a bit before and after school. We'll cope all right.'

'I can help, too,' I said. It seemed that everyone was counting me out. Perhaps it was because I hadn't been much use in the past.

'That's good, Paula,' Dad said. 'All hands to the plough at the moment, eh?' He dozed off again. We sat by his bed and waited till the doctor came and he suggested we should go into the waiting room while he examined Dad. Later he came in and talked to us.

'Fortunately,' he said, 'there's no internal damage. We've had a look at the x-rays, but his back has been badly strained. I understand he's a farmer?'

'Yes,' said Mum.

'Is there anyone you can call on for help? It's going to

be some time before he'll be fit enough for work. I'm talking about months.'

'We have some good neighbours,' said Mum. 'We'll manage all right.'

'We have to be thankful,' she said as we drove home, 'that it wasn't worse. I can cope with the chickens and if Philip takes over the pigs, we should be able to manage, at least for a while.' We had over a thousand head of poultry. They had to be fed twice a day and cleaned out and when the eggs were collected, they had to be graded, cleaned and packed. It was too much for her to take on herself, and I knew that trying to find someone in the village to help, was out of the question. We simply couldn't afford it.

I had been doing some thinking and I intended to speak to Bruce about it, but I wasn't looking forward to it. Even if he understood the reason for my sudden departure, I could hardly expect him to be in a cooperative mood for what I had in mind. I had to be careful because I couldn't afford to lose my job. We needed every penny and I intended to hand over the whole of my wages to Mum.

On Monday morning I set off early for the stables. The horse-box stood in the stable yard, so I knew that Bruce was safely back. I went into Ranger's box and he whinnied softly and nuzzled me.

'Good old boy,' I whispered. 'You did so well but it just didn't turn out right.'

'So you're back,' said Bruce, looking over the door of the loose-box. 'What news of your father?'

'He's badly hurt. The tractor rolled over and he was pinned under the safety bar. He's broken his leg in two places. I want to talk to you about it, Bruce.'

80

'Come into the house for a cup of coffee then.'

I followed him in, wondering how he would take it.

'I'm sorry I had to leave you on your own with the horses,' I began. 'Did you manage all right?'

'Yes. Someone gave me a hand with Ranger. As usual he kicked up a fuss as soon as I got him near the horse-box. Why was it Fletcher who came for you?'

'Matthew's a local farmer and a friend of ours. He's helping us with the cattle now Dad's out of action.'

'Came a long way, didn't he? It could have waited till the next day, surely?'

'It couldn't, Bruce. I wanted to get back and it was good of him to come.'

Bruce shrugged. 'Well, what is it you want to talk about?'

'Mum and Philip can't manage the farm on their own,' I began. 'Phil's got exams and it's all Mum can do to manage the house and visit Dad. I must help them. I want to work part-time, Bruce. I can get most of my work here done in the mornings and still have time to help you with the mail.'

Bruce was thoughtful. 'How long do you reckon this will last?' he asked.

'I honestly don't know. They warned us that it will be some time before Dad's fit to work again, and at the moment, we don't even know if he'll ever be able to. We can only wait and see.'

'I'm sorry to hear that,' said Bruce. 'Real bad luck on him. But as far as your job here goes, it's come at a time when we're particularly busy. I've got this new mare coming in and I want you to start work on her. Besides which, there's more shows coming up and I'm depending

81

on you to ride Ranger. It means a lot of extra work.'

'I'm sure I can manage it. I could work from seven to twelve every day, except Sundays, of course.'

'But can I rely on you?' asked Bruce. 'You may find it's too much with the extra work you're taking on at home and I could be in real trouble without a rider. I'd rather know just where I stand.' He brought out a packet of cigarettes and lit up. 'Besides,' he said, taking a long draw and exhaling, 'I don't have to remind you, that it won't do your career any good if you drop out now. People are beginning to notice you and I heard some encouraging remarks about your riding on Saturday. It's all good publicity for the stables, as well as building up your own reputation. You won't lose sight of that, I hope.'

I didn't want to lose sight of it, but the only thing that mattered to me just now was Dad.

Before I left that evening, Bruce said he was prepared to give it a try but he warned me that it couldn't go on indefinitely.

I thought about it on my way home. I knew Bruce meant what he said and if I failed to turn up because something needed attention at home, he might sack me. I wondered if I would be able to cope with both jobs, and then there was the riding school. I didn't want to give that up just when we'd got it going, but it was a question of priorities.

Mum was in the kitchen when I got back.

'Have you seen Dad?' I asked.

'I went over this afternoon. He's sleeping a lot but that's because of the drugs they're giving him for the pain. I just sat beside him as he didn't seem up to talking.'

'I was going there by bus this evening. Do you think

I should?'

'No, dear. It's a long ride and we'll go tomorrow evening together.'

'I've spoken to Bruce and he's letting me work part-time so that I can help on the farm.'

Mum brightened. 'That'll be a great help, love.'

Matthew came over that evening with a cheque. 'That's what we owe you for grazing fees,' he said. Just like Matthew. Always turning up with something practical just when we needed it and never as though he was doing us a favour. Mum put in into her purse. 'It will come in useful just now. Thanks, Matthew.'

'I thought of running over to the hospital,' said Matthew. 'Want to come, Paula, or have you already been?'

'I'd like to,' I said.

'See you later, then,' said Mum.

On the way I told him that I'd arranged to work part-time so that I could help out at home.

'That will be a relief to your parents,' he said. 'We've got to give some thought to the future as well. For instance what to plant once we've harvested the long meadow. Then to my mind, those young pigs are ready for market, but I reckon Philip understands that side of it.'

He went on about the farm and I listened carefully to what he was saying but it seemed to me that his usual friendly, relaxed attitude had changed and that he kept on about the farm because he didn't want to talk about more personal things. Although he had said nothing about the night he had come to fetch me, it hung between us and I felt he blamed me for what had happened.

I blamed myself too, and I couldn't forgive myself. I

was conscious of it all day long. I tried praying, but I couldn't believe God wanted to listen to me – not after what I'd done. As the days passed, Dad seemed just as ill and I felt sure that God was punishing me for my disobedience.

When we reached the hospital, Dad was sleeping. We waited by his bed and presently he woke up and we talked to him for a while about the farm and tried to reassure him that we had everything under control. But he didn't seem to be taking it in and obviously it was an effort for him to concentrate.

Just before we left, he said, 'I'm sorry I'm not very bright at present. I know how busy you are and I'd rather you didn't waste your time coming to see me. They'll let you know if there's an emergency.'

I lent over and kissed him. 'Dad, I *want* to come and see you. I couldn't bear not to.'

He gave me his old smile then and I had to turn away because I didn't want him to see how upset I was. Matthew took my arm and led me out of the hospital. He didn't start the car right away and we sat in silence for a while.

'He'll be all right,' he said presently. 'He just needs time.'

'But he looks so ill. He seems to have lost interest in everything.'

'That's because he needs to sleep. It's a good thing he isn't worrying about the farm. There's nothing we can do at the moment, Paula, but to keep on praying.'

'I can't pray about it.'

Matthew glanced at me. 'Why not?' he asked.

'I don't know why. I just feel that God's angry with me. He doesn't want to listen.'

'God isn't like that,' said Matthew. 'He's always ready to listen and to help. You can't blame yourself for the accident. That old tractor was dangerous. I think it's something between yourself and your dad that's worrying you. That's something different and it can be put right as soon as he's better.'

I was silent. I expect he was right, but I didn't feel like praying any more. It seemed useless to bring God into it at all.

Presently I said, 'I'd like to believe that God is listening and would make Dad better, but until I have a chance to show him that I'm sorry and try and put things right, I don't think he's interested.'

Matthew turned to me with a smile.

'Paula! You've got it all wrong. No matter what we do, we can never earn God's forgiveness by our own efforts. That's why Jesus died. He took all our sins on himself and paid the price for them, so all we have to do is to say sorry and ask to be forgiven. God loves you and is waiting for you to ask.'

That's what really attracted me – that God loved someone like me so much. It is very hard to turn your back on love.

~9~

I got up early every morning and fed the chickens before I left for work. Now that I was coming home at midday I found that I could manage the poultry myself, besides any other jobs which needed to be done. Another tractor stood in the yard now. Matthew had had the old one taken away and used this one to take food to the cattle and for any heavy work. He was planning to send a combine harvester over to cut our wheat at the same time as theirs and this would save expense. I knew the bills were mounting, but I left this side of it to Matthew and Mum.

Surprisingly, I found that I was enjoying farm work. There was a deep sense of satisfaction in being entirely responsible for the poultry and it was a great feeling that together we were able to keep the wheels turning for Dad.

So far things seemed to be running smoothly at the stables and I was able to get through all my work to Bruce's satisfaction. The new mare had not yet arrived but there were other horses that had to be schooled and by the end of the day I was exhausted. I went to bed at nine o'clock and slept right through till the alarm woke me at six in the morning.

The following Sunday the children came down again. All the helpers had heard about Dad and turned up in good time with their ponies. More offers of help were always coming in and we considered each carefully. Any unsuitable ones were politely turned down with words to the effect that we might be able to make use of them some time in the future.

This was the children's third visit and they were already gaining confidence. They went straight to the ponies and were so eager to begin that we had to restrain them. We went over the things we had done on their last visit, showing them how to groom and muck out the ponies and they watched as we put on the saddles and bridles. Everything had to be taken slowly, one step at a time.

At last they were allowed to mount and we helped them onto the ponies, reminding them of the correct position and how to hold the reins. I led Billy slowly round the ring, a helper on either side of him. He found balancing very difficult and lurched from side to side which quickly tired him. He asked if he could get down and was perfectly happy standing close to Brigand and talking to him.

As I took off the saddle, he suddenly said, 'I told my mum about you. I want to come and live 'ere with you.'

I laughed. 'I don't expect she'd want you to do that, Billy. She'd miss you.'

'No. She's got them others.'

'How many?'

'Five of us.'

'She must have her hands full. What about your dad?'

'I ain't got no dad. Me mum goes out to work.'

'Are you the youngest?' I asked. I was interested in this little boy.

'Yeah. Me sister looked after me but she's in care now.' Billy was a mine of information.

'Why's that?'

'She got caught for pinching. We was always short cos Mum ain't got much so Sis used to nick things for us.'

'So who looks after you now?' I asked.

'I goes to a neighbour when Mum's out. I 'ates it. I likes the country and all them animals. Can I come and live 'ere then?'

'No, Billy. I work too, and I wouldn't be able to look after you. Besides, you have to go to school. But you can come down again to ride, can't you?'

He didn't seem too sure. 'Dunno,' he said. 'They make promises and they don't always keep 'em. If I lived 'ere, I'd be OK. I won't be no trouble. Honest I won't.'

I thought a lot about Billy after that. I was determined that whatever happened I would continue with these sessions. It was great to be able to do something for these kids.

When it was over, Don thanked me. 'They're talking about this place all the time,' he said, watching the children with the ponies. 'It's added a new dimension to their lives and it's given them confidence. They seem to be behaving better, too.'

'They behave very well,' I said.

'They're doing what they like to do here, that's why. But in their daily routine they get bitterly frustrated by their limitations and throw tantrums and refuse to cooperate. It takes a lot of time and patience to help them.'

'I can understand that. It's a pity they can't come down here more often, but I'm afraid we couldn't manage it.'

'You're doing enough,' said Don, 'and very grateful we are. I've always held the view that children need animals and I'm beginning to think that an association with ponies and horses is ideal for these kids. Some of them are going to have a hard time when they leave school, with problems of fitting into the community and finding a job and I have an idea that through horses they could learn to be independent, at least to some extent. You can see that they respond to ponies in a way that they never respond to an adult. It's a subject I'm interested in and I want to find out more about it.'

'But you're talking about children with behaviour problems, aren't you? Not these children with physical disabilities?'

'I'm talking about both. I think children of all ages, particularly young adults with emotional problems and perhaps with other disabilities, could benefit from an association with horses at an age when they won't accept help from anyone else.'

It was an intriguing idea. 'A lot of research would have to be done on it, surely,' I said. 'If they were really to benefit they would need a much closer association with the animals. They would have to live and work with them to have any real effect and there can't be many places that would cater for that.'

'I believe there is a riding centre somewhere in the New Forest that does something like this, but I don't know much about it.'

'If you ever find out, please let me know,' I said.

When they'd gone, Jenny asked if I'd go round to her place for the afternoon.

'I'm afraid I can't,' I said. 'I've got work to do here.'

'Then I'll help you,' she said. 'I wanted to do something to help and here's my chance.'

I grinned at her. Together we cleared away the posts and mounting blocks and then we had lunch. Afterwards she helped me pack the eggs. These had to be done every day if I was to keep pace with it all.

'When will your dad be coming home?' she asked.

'They haven't told us yet.'

'It was a ghastly thing to happen. You read about these tractor accidents but you never think it's going to happen to someone you know. You were away at the time, weren't you?'

'Yes. I was riding at a show in the Midlands and Matthew came and brought me back.' Suddenly I was telling her all about it, my awful feelings of guilt, my arguments with Dad. 'I should never have gone,' I ended.

'Of course you should,' said Jenny. 'It's your job and it was a great opportunity. You proved it, didn't you, by winning? Whether you were right to stay on is another matter. Sounds to me as though you'd have had trouble with Bruce if you had. That's what your dad was worried about, I expect, but he couldn't give you this reason before you left or you'd have flown off the handle.'

'I guess you're right. That makes it all the worse. I feel awful about it, Jenny. He was probably worrying about me and not giving his mind to the tractor when it happened. You see, I deliberately disobeyed him, and I've never done that before.'

'Seems to me,' said Jenny, looking at me sympathetically with her big brown eyes, 'that you had an awful
decision to make between your career and doing what
your dad wanted. Most people of our age would have
done what you did. I think perhaps I would myself, but
I would have prayed about it first. I always do when I
can't make up my mind about something.'

'Then God might have made it quite clear that I wasn't
to go. Then what would I have done? How can you
possibly tell whether God wants you to do something
or not? You've got to figure it out for yourself.'

'It's not always easy, but you're usually pretty certain
about the answer. It might not be what you want, but
when you think about it, it makes sense. God isn't a
spoil-sport. He knows how keen you are to do well.
After all, he gave you this ability to ride. You're really
good, Paula. Surely if we're given talents, we should
make full use of them.'

'I'm not sure, Jenny. Not when it hurts someone. Dad
didn't want to stop me riding. He was only trying to
protect me from the sort of thing he thought went on
after the show.'

Dad was slowly improving and he was having physiotherapy daily. They said if he continued to make progress, he could soon come home, but they warned us
that he would need a lot of support. He was fretting
about the farm now, which was a good sign, but it
would be a long time before he could do anything himself. Although we wanted him home, I was worried that
it would make a lot of extra work for Mum.

Philip's exams were coming up, too, and Mum and
Dad insisted that he must take them, even if he was

going to farm. His teachers had warned him that unless he was prepared to get down to studying, he would fail. I told him I'd take over his work but I was finding that I couldn't cope with everything in the time available. Sometime soon, I'd have to talk to Bruce again. I dreaded this and kept putting it off.

Then I turned up one morning to find two changes in the stables. The chestnut colt had gone and in his place was a grey mare. She was a lovely animal, part Arab, with small ears and wide, gentle eyes.

'Isn't she a beauty?' said Bruce, as I stood gazing at her. 'She'll jump anything.'

'When did these changes take place?' I asked him.

'The colt left on Saturday and Silver Mist came in yesterday. I fixed it up in Derbyshire when we were there.'

I was silent. I was thinking that in the horse world, things changed so quickly. You had a super horse that you worked with and loved and it trusted you, but if someone offered a good price, it was sold. It might not be badly treated because of its value, but there were many ways of training horses and sometimes they could be cruel. In my opinion the only way to train an animal was to build up trust and then it would do anything for you. It was something I'd noticed with the children. They trusted those ponies and the ponies responded.

'We've got to work on this mare,' said Bruce, interrupting my thoughts. 'I intend to enter her for the West Counties show next month and I'm depending on you for that. You're just the right weight for her.'

'I don't know whether I can,' I said. 'I want to talk to you about it, Bruce.'

'What is it this time?' he asked, impatience creeping

into his voice.

'Dad's coming home but he can't work and unless I'm there full time, we just can't manage. My brother's got exams and Mum's going to be fully occupied with Dad. I'm sorry because I feel I'm letting you down.'

Bruce swore. 'You can say that again. I thought we'd been through all that when I asked you to let me know earlier if you wanted to leave. I have to plan ahead and now where am I going to find another rider at this late stage? You know and understand these horses. It would take months to train someone else.'

He was right and I didn't know what to say. There seemed no alternative. If I'd been able to talk it over with Dad, he might have advised me, but I didn't want to do this. It would only worry him.

'Perhaps I could come and work with the horses sometimes, so that I could ride in the shows. Would that help?'

'Emphatically not! I agreed to your suggestion for part-time work and that seems to be all right, but less than that is useless. Unless I can depend on you for at least a few days each week, I'll have to look round for someone else.'

At that moment I saw my career floating away. It was no good telling him that it was only temporary because now I couldn't see an end to the situation. I had to be prepared to work full-time on the farm indefinitely. It was going to be terribly hard to cut horses out of my life, the glamour of the show ring in exchange for the drudgery of farming.

Bruce must have noticed my hesitation, because he said, 'Think it over tonight and let me know tomorrow. I've got to be straight with you, Paula. I've told you before, if you're going to follow your career, it's got to be whole-hearted. Can't you find someone else to help on the farm?'

I shook my head. We couldn't afford it.

I was about to leave, when he suddenly said, 'Like to try the mare before you go?'

I looked at my watch. I should be back to feed the animals, but they'd have to wait a little longer.

He saddled the mare and helped me to mount. I took her into the ring. It was like walking on air, her movements were so smooth, her ears pricked and eager, ready to respond to every touch.

'Try her over a couple of jumps,' said Bruce.

She sailed over them. She was all the chestnut colt had promised to be and more. She was a dream.

Bruce, watching, said, 'You're just right for each other, Paula. Together you'd be unbeatable. Come to think of it, she might even be the right horse for you, but her price is high.'

I went home without giving him my final word. He insisted that I should think it over and now there was the added temptation of the mare. I didn't know what to do.

It was long past feeding time for the pigs and I hurried into the barn to mix their food where I found Matthew.

'I've fed them,' he said. 'I came over to look at the cattle and your mum was worried because you weren't back.'

'Thanks,' I said. 'I got held up at the stables.'

He gave me a long look and I knew what he was thinking, but he would never say so. He thought that I preferred to spend my time there, in spite of the fact that there was more urgent work to be done here. He would just have to think on. I didn't feel like explaining myself to anyone. In the old days, I might have talked to him about the job, but not now. He wouldn't see it my way. Horses meant nothing to him and running the farm was everything.

For the rest of the day I turned it over in my mind and I kept thinking about the grey mare. I knew with a horse like that, I could win the big prizes. I might even reach national level. I thought all ways round it, but so long as I was trying to do both jobs, I could do neither properly and I seemed to be upsetting everyone. I thought of talking to Jenny about it, but I just didn't have the time. I remembered what she'd said though.

That night, no nearer a decision and feeling very self-conscious, I knelt down by my bed and asked God what I should do about it. I didn't think I would be able to pray, but I soon forgot myself and found it was like talking to a friend who already knew and understood it all. I felt that God was very close to me at that moment and that, far from condemning me, he loved me and wanted to help. I thanked him for giving Dad back to us and I asked him to forgive me for all the selfish things I'd done.

I went on to tell him how hard it would be to give up all hope of competitive riding just when I was doing well, but I said I'd do it if he'd help me, because I didn't think I could do it on my own. I stayed on my knees for a long time after this, thinking about him and then I got into bed and read my old school copy of the Bible until I went to sleep.

I expected to wake up with a clear understanding of what to say to Bruce, but that didn't happen. I went off to feed the animals and gave it further thought. Perhaps, after all, it was quite simple. Unless I gave up the job, we couldn't manage. Matthew was putting in more time at the farm than he could afford and that wasn't fair. Phil was working when he should have been studying and soon, when Dad came home, Mum would have her hands full and would need my help. So, no matter what, I had to do it. If I turned my back on it now, I wouldn't be able to live with myself.

'Well', said Bruce, when I arrived, 'have you had a think about your future?'

'Yes,' I said. 'Could you find someone to take my place here?'

His face darkened. 'I think you're making a big mistake,' he said.

'I've thought about it a lot. I'm sorry and I shall always be grateful for the chance you gave me. I hope you'll find someone soon and if I can help occasionally, I will.'

If I had hoped to keep some contact with the stables, this was quickly dashed.

'There's no need,' said Bruce. 'I had a phone call last night. A very promising young rider wants to come here to train. She's ready to start immediately, so you can leave with a free conscience.'

At the end of the morning he gave me a cheque which brought my pay up to date and I said good-bye.

Then, turning my back on my dreams and my future and the beautiful silver mare that someone else would now ride, I left.

~10~

Strange though it seemed, I was far from miserable. Now I had the whole day, I worked at a steady pace and didn't get so tired. I loved those early summer mornings with the dew on the grass and the sun coming up over the hills to the east. Bess was my constant companion and followed me everywhere. I had more time to talk to Mum, too. I realised that she had been left very much on her own lately and we were able to share the visits to Dad.

I had been thinking, too, about my promise to God. Matthew had said that it made a difference to your life but I felt just the same. I talked to Jenny about it.

'I don't feel any different,' I told her. 'If anything, I'm a bit scared. I've made this promise which I must try to keep and I've no idea what to expect.'

Jenny smiled . 'You're reckoning without God,' she said. 'He's already accepted you and now you belong to him. He'll take your prayer seriously. It's really exciting,

Paula. I'm so thrilled about it.'

I smiled ruefully, hardly understanding her enthusiasm. I didn't see that it was such a big deal.

'Would you like us to pray together about it?' she asked.

'Perhaps it would be a good idea,' I said. I felt embarrassed and I didn't know what Jenny expected of me, let alone God.

'Then let's sit quietly together.' Jenny sat there with her eyes closed, quite silent for a while, then she began to pray. 'Thank you, Father, that you have brought Paula into your family. You love her and you understand her fears. Please encourage her because it's quite hard when you become a Christian and you don't know what to expect. Thank you that you gave your dear son, Jesus Christ, so that our sins are forgiven. Amen.'

I said 'Amen' and that was it. Jenny looked at me.

'Don't expect anything spectacular,' she said. 'It doesn't happen like that, but whenever you want to talk about it, I'll do my best.'

After that I felt happier. I had a lot to learn, but I was glad that I had made that promise. I was lucky to have friends like Jenny and Matthew who could help me. It must be quite difficult for people who wanted to become Christians but had no idea how to go about it and no one to share it with.

One evening when it was almost dark and I was locking up the chickens, I saw Matthew coming across the field.

'Your mother told me I'd find you here,' he said. 'She said you'd given up your job at the stables.'

'That's right. I couldn't manage both and with Dad coming home, I'm really needed here. I wanted to thank you, Matthew, for all you've done for us. We couldn't have managed without you.'

'Nonsense. I'm glad to help. Your dad's done a lot for us in the past one way and another. He taught me a lot about farming, too – things that people don't set much store by these days. Some would call them old fashioned ideas, watching signs in the countryside that tell you about weather conditions, or the look of an animal when something's bothering him, those sorts of things. Your father's a wise man, Paula.'

'I know that now. I'd never given it much thought before.'

'What are you going to do when all this is over?' asked Matthew. 'Going back to show jumping?'

'I don't know. I haven't planned that far ahead.'

'That job was important to you, wasn't it, Paula? How do you feel about giving it up?'

'I haven't had much time to think about it, but when I do, it's not as bad as I thought it was going to be.'

'It couldn't have been easy,' said Matthew. 'You were never that keen on farming and yet you gave up something you really wanted to do so that you could keep things going for your dad.'

'I'm glad you're not blaming me any more, Matthew.' I couldn't resist a dig at him.

'I never blamed you. I knew it was difficult for you and that you were unhappy but whenever I wanted to talk about it, you clammed up. Does your dad know about the job?'

'I don't think so. It would only upset him and make him feel he ought to get back to work before he's ready.'

In fact, when Dad came home, one of the first things he said to me was, 'Mum told me you'd left the stables to help out. It was a big decision for you to take on your own, love, and I'm grateful to you. I don't think we could have managed any other way.'

He was walking about on sticks and almost immediately he insisted on taking a look round the yard, with Mum and me badgering him about not overdoing it and resting. He seemed satisfied with our report and, although his back still gave him a lot of pain and he had to go back to the hospital twice a week for physiotherapy, he seemed quite cheerful.

The date of the West Counties show came and went and I heard nothing from Bruce, so I gathered his new rider had turned out all right. Although I looked through the local papers, I could see no report on the show and I didn't feel like asking. It was better to cut all connections with the stables and it was only sometimes that I thought about the grey mare and wondered about the girl who was riding her now. And, just occasionally, I hoped that Bruce didn't think so highly of her as he did of me.

The Sunday after Dad came out, the children came down again. The ponies we'd selected for the job had proved their value and the children loved them. Mrs Owen was fantastic. She turned up to all the sessions and always insisted on a meeting between times so we could go over any problems and find ways of keeping the lessons interesting enough as well as therapeutic.

This time Billy brought his own carrot with him and he went over to Brigand, holding it flat in his hand. The pony took it gently and chomped but with the bit in his mouth he found it difficult to eat.

'Let's take the bridle off,' I said, slipping it over his head. When the carrot was finished, I showed Billy how to put the bridle on again and he managed to do up the straps. I was worried because he had a nasty deep cough.

'Have you got a cold?' I asked him.

'No. I always cough. If it ain't no better next time, they won't bring me.' Billy's eyes were full of anguish.

'Then we must see that it is better,' I said, and made a mental note to speak to Don about it.

Billy soon got tired. It was quite an effort for him to get his two small legs across Brigand's back and in the right position and soon he asked if he could get down. We helped him off and then he asked if he could see the river.

I hesitated. If the other children heard, they'd all want to come. 'How do you know about the river?' I asked him.

'Don said you had a river. I like rivers.'

I doubted whether he'd ever seen any river other than the Thames, but I saw no reason why we shouldn't wander down there while the others were riding.

As we crossed the field, Billy took my hand. 'I asked me mum if I could come and live with you,' he said.

'And what did she say?'

'She said I could if I wanted. If I could,' he looked up eagerly into my face, 'I'd get better. I know I would.'

I thought there might be some truth in that, but I had to dissuade him firmly, otherwise he'd be hankering after it.

'Billy, I'd love it if you came to live with us, but it's impossible. My mum and dad are busy and I have to work, so there'd be no one to look after you. You've got your family and your nice school and lots of children to play with. You wouldn't have any of those here and you'd be very lonely.'

'Is that the river?' His mind had raced on.

'Yes, where that line of trees are.'

He hurried ahead, swinging his lame leg out sideways and the effort brought on another bout of coughing.

'Cor,' he said. 'It's a titchy little stream. Our river's much bigger.'

'Yes,' I agreed.

'But I like this one best. It's secret and wild.'

'It's very secret. There now, if you sit down quietly on the bank and keep still, we might see a few things.'

There was a plop in the water. 'A fish!' squealed Billy. 'I saw a fish!'

'Ssh. We'll see more if you don't make a noise.'

He kept very quiet and still then, absorbed in his surroundings. There was a regular tapping in an oak tree on the other side of the river and presently the bird made its way round the tree.

'See, Billy,' I whispered. 'It's a green woodpecker.'

'Yeah. I sees 'im,' said Billy. Then I looked downstream and slowly, like a stately galleon, a swan came into sight and glided right past us. Billy was estatic.

'You see them in London, don't you?' I reminded him.

'Yeah, but not like 'im. 'Ee's magic.' Then, the next moment, his mate sailed past, followed by five cygnets. It was as though the sight had been laid on specially for him.

'There now,' I said presently. 'I think perhaps we'd better get back. The others will be wondering where we are.'

He came slowly, whether to prolong the walk, or because by now he was very tired indeed, I wasn't sure. But I didn't hurry him. I felt this short time had provided him with hours of interest and happy memories for when he got back home. It was something he could tell his friends and perhaps, for the first time in his life, he had something to boast about.

'I reckon God lives 'ere',' he said suddenly. 'It's sort of like 'eaven, ain't it?'

'He doesn't only live in beautiful places, Billy. He lives in cities and in poor places. He's everywhere.'

'But I know 'e's 'ere,' said Billy. 'I can feel 'im.'

'He's with you all the time, wherever you are. He wants to look after you.'

Billy looked at me with interest. 'I'd like 'im to make me better, so I could do wot them others do. Do you reckon 'e could?'

I was getting out of my depth. 'I don't know, Billy, but I do know that he loves you very much, and he doesn't want you to be unhappy. There are lots of sick and sad people about, in fact most of us are at some time or other, and if we ask God to help us, he will. Perhaps he won't make us well. I don't know why not, but he's promised to be with us, even when we're ill or frightened. Do you understand, Billy?'

'Yeah,' said Billy, doubtfully. 'Why can't we see 'im, then?'

'I don't know, but we can get to know him and trust him, but first we have to tell him we want him to be our friend. He won't come unless we ask him. But if we do, even if we can only give him a tiny place in our hearts, he will fill it with his love and it spreads until other people feel it, too.'

'The size of a pea?' asked Billy.

'What I meant was it depends on how important he is to us. If everything else in our lives is more important to us than him, then we're not giving him much room and he can't do much for us. But if we love him very much and give him lots of room, then he can do all sorts of wonderful things for us and make us very happy.'

'Then he can have all the room I've got,' said Billy. The next moment he had lost interest. 'I think I'll have another ride,' he said.

The others were still concentrating on the lesson and hadn't noticed our absence. While Billy was talking to Brigand, I had a word with Don.

'He's got a nasty cough,' I told him. 'He says it gets worse in winter.'

'Yes, it does. He's a frail little fellow, but quite wiry. These visits have done him the world of good. He talks about them all the time.'

'He's terrified that he might not make it next time. He says you won't let him come if his cough gets bad.'

'No, we can't take the risk. It could easily turn to bronchitis.'

'It would break his heart if the others came and he had to stay behind.'

'We'll take good care of him, don't worry. Come the autumn, a lot of them fall prey to all sorts of illness. They don't get a particularly good diet at home and many of them lack the care they need.'

When they'd gone, I felt that warm glow I always felt with these children. It struck me that it was something like winning in the show ring, but the prizes were different. They were hidden and had to be searched for, coming in the form of a smile from Billy when he tucked his hand into mine, or a shy thank-you from one of the other children.

I thought a lot about my conversation with Billy. I knew my answers to his questions had been very inadequate and had meant little to him, but I felt that God was very close to these children and that he didn't depend on my own poor explanations. The children were able to find him for themselves. I spoke to Matthew about it one day when he was over.

'It's so difficult to answer his questions,' I told him. 'I want to make promises for God, like telling Billy that if he prays, he'll be cured because that's what he wants more than anything. But I can't say that, so I have to try and make him understand that God loves him very much and that he will help him in other ways. I don't think he saw much sense in that.'

'We make it sound so complicated,' said Matthew, 'when it should be so beautifully simple. We don't always recognise this longing most of us have to know God. It doesn't seem logical to us, but I think it's often stronger in a child. Billy seems to want to know him, even if he doesn't understand why. That's good enough for God and their relationship will develop from there.'

Matthew's words were convincing, but I thought Billy and his friends would have difficulty in understanding. I could only hope that some of the things of which Billy and I had spoken that day, would make sense to him and would be a beginning on which his faith might grow.

~11~

Autumn came early that year and the countryside was touched with reds and golds. The great combine harvester had cut the field of wheat. It was a rich crop and would bring in much needed cash. Now the field stood covered in stubble, waiting to be ploughed and replanted. Dad had negotiated with the insurance company over the tractor and had come to an agreement with Matthew. It wasn't new, but it was a great improvement on the old one. Dad spent a lot of his time in the yard, inspecting the engine. It was hard to restrain him now that he was so keen to get back to work.

Philip and I managed quite well between us, without too many arguments. I tried to go along with his ideas because he was, after all, going to be the one to stay on the farm. He had done all right in his exams, but nothing would persuade him to go back to school for another two years. He wanted to start work straight away. Dad had always intended that he should go to agricultural college, but that was out of the question now, so Dad got round to thinking that a couple of years on the farm might stand him in good stead, by which time he could think about college.

The time was coming when I would no longer be needed here and Dad was keen that I should make plans for the future.

'You've been a tremendous help, Paula, but we'll soon be able to manage and you'll be free to think about your own future. Bruce will be expecting you back at the stables. He's been very patient.' I hadn't told him that Bruce had taken on someone else and I'd lost my opportunity there.

'I don't know, Dad. I haven't made up my mind yet.'

'Seems to me you've taken to farming. There's room for all of us, you know. You could do your own thing, a few calves, sheep, something like that, or you might want to enlarge on the riding side of it. Start your own business, eh?'

I smiled at him. 'Two in the family are enough, but I'll think about it.'

I had been doing a lot of thinking and I was sure that I didn't want to work on the farm. Maybe I could enlarge the school, but that would mean building stables and anyway it wasn't what I had in mind. It was these children that fascinated me. To see their enthusiasm and affection for the ponies and watch their progress was thrilling. They were as proud as punch when they tackled something on their own for the first time and you could see their confidence growing. But if I was to do this properly, and become established, I would have to undergo some sort of training and I had no idea where.

Somehow it didn't bother me too much. I had a feeling

that when the time came, I would know the right thing to do. I talked to Jenny about it.

'Are you praying about it?' asked Jenny, bluntly.

'Yes.' I found these days it was much easier to pray, specially if I was worried about something, and quite often before I went to sleep, I read the Bible. I was finding it really interesting and time and again I came across passages that answered questions I had been asking myself. I liked the gospels best, the life of Jesus, and I could understand now why people like Jenny and Matthew wanted to follow his teaching.

'Then you'll get your answer,' said Jenny firmly. 'Not perhaps when you expect it, because God doesn't spell it out, but when the time comes, you'll know. If you need the answer today, you'll have it today, but if you don't need it till next Wednesday, you'll have it then. You have to give it a lot of thought, of course, but I'm sure that if we ask him, God guides our thoughts when decisions have to be made.'

'I feel I need to get away for a while,' I said. 'We've been so busy here through the summer and I couldn't make any plans before I knew if Dad was going to be all right and Philip's exam results were OK.'

'I think you should,' said Jenny. 'Why don't you enjoy yourself for a while? You're always thinking about other people and it's time you had yourself a bit of fun.'

'Which we're going to do on Saturday,' I said. 'You're coming to Matthew's barn dance, aren't you?'

Matthew had invited Philip and myself to the Young Farmers' Harvest Supper and Barn Dance and as usual it was held on the Saturday preceding the Harvest Festival service.

It was great to get out of my old farm clothes. I seemed

to have worn nothing but jeans or riding breeches for months and now it was a real treat to put on my pretty blue dress and a new pair of sandals Mum had bought me. I dressed with care and brushed my long, fair hair until it shone and fell thickly about my shoulders.

The big barn with the lovely old tiled roof and great beams was full of young people when we arrived and there were a lot of faces I recognised. Matthew had fixed up some coloured lights round the barn and it looked very festive. On one side was a long table laden with food and fruit and great loaves of bread and on another table stood flagons of cider together with bottles of Mrs Fletcher's elderflower champagne. A band which was made up of local musicians was playing popular numbers. Jenny was there with her violin, someone else had a guitar and Matthew's brother played the flute. They had borrowed the old piano from the pub and although it hadn't been tuned for years, the church organist strummed away in merry mood.

Matthew came over and asked me for the first dance. 'You look absolutely stunning, Paula.' It seemed that everyone had got so used to seeing me in working clothes that they were surprised to see me dressed up.

'Help yourself to the food,' he invited. I joined the queue and was soon talking to some people I hadn't seen for years. I felt myself more part of the scene than ever before. Perhaps it was because now I knew something about farming and had really earned my place there. Lots of people had heard about Dad and enquired about him.

After supper the tables and benches were pushed back and when the music struck up again, people formed eights for the first dance. Matthew quickly explained the general idea, but most of us knew the dances from past years; those new to it soon got the hang of it. Matthew and I were the lead couple and everyone followed us. It was great and as the pace grew hotter and we exchanged partners down the line, all shyness disappeared as we threw ourselves into the dance. No sooner had I sat down, hot and breathless, than someone asked me for the next dance and so on through the evening. I hadn't enjoyed myself so much in years.

'Keep the last dance for me, will you?' said Matthew, 'or I'll never get a look in.'

We danced on till well past midnight and then everyone joined hands and sang Auld Lang Syne. Philip had disappeared with Kirsty, a local farmer's daughter with whom he'd been dancing all the evening, so I stayed for a while to help with the clearing up. Then Matthew said he'd run me home. I followed him out to the car and he held the door open for me.

'It was a super evening, Matthew. I've never enjoyed it so much.'

'You've never been more part of it, that's why,' said Matthew. 'Everyone knows what you've been doing on the farm and they think a lot of you for helping out when your dad was ill.'

'I enjoyed it,' I said. 'I've learnt a lot and anyway we couldn't have done it without you.'

'But you wouldn't want to spend the rest of your life on a farm?'

I laughed. 'I don't think so. I want to get away for a while. Do something different, but I don't know what.'

We had reached the house and Matthew stopped the car in the yard and switched off the lights. I started to get out when he stopped me and, putting his arm round me, drew me gently towards him and kissed me.

It stirred in me feelings which I had never associated with Matthew. I had grown so used to him and missed him when he wasn't there. Sometimes I had seen him looking at me with an expression in his eyes which I didn't want to face up to because I wasn't sure of my own feelings for him. I wasn't ready for a new relationship with him, but now I found myself responding to his kisses.

'I've wanted to do that for a long time,' he said, 'and it was just as wonderful as I imagined it would be.'

'Oh Matthew. I didn't expect that.'

'Do you mean to tell me that you'd never thought about it before? You didn't seem entirely surprised and it seems to me that you didn't mind.'

'I liked it,' I admitted, 'but don't let's take it too seriously.'

He laughed. 'All right. I get the message. You don't want to be rushed, but just the same, I'm telling you that I like you a lot, Paula, and I want you to know it.'

'You've always been a super friend and I don't think I want that to change.'

'It doesn't have to. It's simply building on that relationship.'

'Yes, but it takes some getting used to.'

'Of course, and for the moment, I'll be satisfied if you try.'

'Do you want to come in for coffee or something?' I asked him, avoiding an answer.

He shook his head. 'No, thanks. I've got to get back to help with the clearing up, but I'll be seeing you soon, Paula.' And, with another kiss, he let me get out of the car.

I lay in bed, too excited by the evening's events to sleep.

I thought of Matthew's kisses and my own reaction to them. Matthew was a great person and most girls would have given anything to be in my shoes, but I wasn't ready for a steady relationship with anyone at the moment. It only added to the problems I was trying to resolve.

When, at last, I fell asleep, it seemed only a few moments before the alarm went off and I had to get up. The children were coming down again today and we had to get the ponies ready.

It was a cool autumn day and the sun was trying to break through the clouds as I stood watching the children getting out of the bus. But, this time, Billy was not among them.

'Where's Billy?' I asked Don.

'He's got bronchitis, I'm afraid,' he said, 'and there was no way we could bring him. Of course he was disappointed but I think he felt too ill to care much. I went round to see him and promised that if he's better, he can come next time.'

I felt Billy's disappointment keenly. His worst fears were realised and he must have been wondering when he'd ever feel well enough to come again. I went inside the house and found a card with a picture of a pony on it. In it I wrote, 'To dear Billy, Brigand is sad you couldn't come this time and so am I, but we are waiting for you, so get well soon, Lots of love, Paula.'

I took it to Don. 'Please could you see that Billy gets this,' I asked him.

'Sure I will,' he said.

Four days later I had a telephone call. As soon as I heard Don's voice, I knew something was wrong.

'Paula? I'm afraid I have some bad news for you.'

'It's Billy, isn't it?'

'Yes. He got pneumonia and died last night.'

'Oh no! How could it happen to him?' I struggled to keep my voice under control.

'It was always on the cards, every winter. He had a real battle and he was a courageous little fellow.'

'I can't believe it, Don. I shall miss him terribly.'

'We all will. There's something else I have to tell you. He told his mum about you and just before he died, he said what you'd told him was true. She felt that she should pass this message on. Does it mean anything to you?'

'Oh yes, it does. Thanks Don.'

Blindly I left the house and walked across the field to the river. My steps took me the way Billy and I had gone that other Sunday. It was a day like this, but now it was evening and everything looked radiant. I paused where Billy and I had sat on the bank. The sun was filtering through the autumn leaves onto the water and there, upstream, was the swan. It seemed that there was no sadness, only a joy and a deep feeling of peace. I felt as though Billy was very close, his weak, disabled body discarded for ever.

I was so thankful that whatever it was I said to him, had been something he could hold onto while he was ill. I could hardly remember what it was, but I realised that is how God works. He gives us the right words when the time comes and they may seem quite inadequate to us, but they're the right words that he wants us to use, the right words for that person at that particular time.

But I missed him terribly. I returned to the house to find Matthew's car in the yard. I didn't feel like talking to anyone at that moment and went into Shelly's loose-box and buried my face in her mane.

It was there that Matthew found me.

'What's the matter, Paula?' He put his hands on my shoulders and turned me towards him. Tears were streaming down my face. 'It's Billy,' I said. 'He's dead.'

'Not the little chap who comes riding? How did it happen?'

'Pneumonia. It's so unfair, Matthew. He only had seven years and they weren't very happy ones. I think the only real happiness was when he came down here. He loved it so much.'

'You must feel pleased that you were able to do that for him,' said Matthew, offering me his handkerchief.

'He kept asking if he could come and live with us. I wonder if he had, whether, with good country air and food, he might have lived.'

'I doubt it. A winter here can be pretty harsh. Besides he wouldn't have been happy. He saw it at its best, the warm days of summer when everything looked beautiful and the ponies were fit and contented. That's how he remembered it.'

He put his arm round my shoulders. 'We get angry sometimes when we don't see sense in things. We have to accept that life is rarely a bed of roses for any of us, but we're journeying towards something far better. Billy's reached it already.'

~12~

The following Sunday I took Shelly out. Now I had more time, I was giving her regular exercise and I enjoyed these rides as much as she did. We went for miles over the heath and through woods until we reached the gentle slopes that led to the downs.

I had just got back and was taking off her saddle, when I heard a car drive into the yard, and the next moment I saw Bruce walking towards me.

'Hullo there,' he said. 'I was coming your way and thought I'd drop in. How are things with you? Your dad on the mend?'

'Yes, he's much better but he still has to take it slowly.'

It was good to see Bruce again. I had avoided going to the stables, but I had often thought about the horses. There was still a part of me that longed to be on a thoroughbred, sizing up its character and why it acted the way it did. The challenge of those big jumps and the feel of a powerful animal gathering itself for the leap, still fascinated me. There was the competitive side of it, too, that appealed to me and the determination to do that bit better than anyone else.

'Still working on the farm, are you?' Bruce asked.

'For the time being.'

I was trying to heave a bale of hay into the stables. Bruce took it from me. 'Let me do it. Where do you want it?'

'Over there, please.'

'What are your plans, then, when your dad's better?'

'I haven't decided yet. At the moment I'm needed here. How are things going at Studlands?' I asked. 'I saw in the local paper you'd had some successes. Congratulations.'

'We've had a few, but I'm sorry you haven't been with us. I believe we could have done better.'

It was nice to hear that, but I knew Bruce was an outrageous flatterer when it suited him.

'How's the grey mare shaping up?'

'She's got tremendous potential. I'm not too fussed about this year. She's on the young side and I'm setting my sights on next season. Actually, Paula, I wondered if you'd be interested in coming back to us?'

'But you said . . .'

'I know. You put me on the spot leaving at short notice like that.'

'But this girl . . .'

'Didn't work out.' Bruce took out a cigarette and lit up. 'To be honest she wasn't a patch on you. Look, I know you can't put in a full week at the moment, but perhaps you could come up from time to time to keep in touch. What do you say?'

It was tempting. In fact, it was rather what I'd hoped

for, that I could do some schooling to keep my hand in, at least until I found a horse of my own to train and, with Bruce's help and encouragement, I could continue my show-jumping career. I would be living at home and available to lend a hand on the farm if I was needed, and it would be nice to be near Matthew. More important, I could continue with the children's riding sessions. I could hardly believe that Bruce was inviting me to come back on my terms and yet, I hesitated. Did I really want to work for him again? A few months back I would have jumped at the opportunity but now, I wasn't sure. Even as Bruce waited confidently for my answer, I was thinking of excuses.

'I don't know, Bruce. I'll have to think about it. In any case, it wouldn't be just yet. Dad still needs me here.'

'I'd make it worth your while,' Bruce pressed. 'You'd get a substantial rise and part of any winnings. I don't have to remind you that our horses equal those you'd find in the best stables in the country and we're investing more money in some really good animals. What we need now are the right riders and those aren't easy to come by.' He gave me a smile which I didn't altogether like. It made me feel that he might be including me in his personal plans and I wasn't interested.

'I'll let you know,' I said.

His face hardened. He wasn't used to being crossed.

'I'd like to have some idea of how you feel about it,' he said. 'You understand, of course, that I have to make plans and I can't wait indefinitely.'

'So you want to know now?' I asked.

'Yes. I want some commitment from you. A week, a month, whatever?'

If he was hoping to rush me into a promise, it wasn't going to work. I realised then that Bruce wasn't going to change and that his only interest in me was my value to the stables.

'All right, Bruce. I understand you need to know, but I have to turn down your offer. I can't commit myself at the moment.'

I don't think he could believe his ears. He stood staring at me, a puzzled expression on his face, then he turned on his heels and, without another word, left.

Thoughtfully, I rubbed Shelly down. I had surprised myself by my answer. I felt certain I was right, but I couldn't help wondering what I was going to do now. I had eliminated one job and I was no nearer having any idea what I was going to do.

I led Shelly down to the paddock and, turning her loose, I went indoors. Mum and Dad were in the sitting room watching television. It was coming up to news time and I sat down to watch. Some sort of appeal was on and a man was talking about a place in the New Forest where residential courses were held, using horses as a means of educating and rehabilitating handicapped and disturbed young people. They also had riding facilities for children with handicaps.

This must be the place that Don was talking about. I made a mental note of the name and address and rushed off to write it down. I had to go and see them. Ever since Don had told me about it and I had seen for myself how the ponies and children responded to each other with love and confidence, I wanted to learn more about it. Besides, I was sure that they would be able to give me some advice on how to run our own small project.

When I told Mrs Owen about it, she was enthusiastic

and said she'd run me down in her car. I rang and made an appointment and the following week we went down to see them.

The Centre was well laid out with stables and a large indoor riding school, surrounded by paddocks and woodlands. Nearby was a residential area with accommodation for thirty young students, all of whom suffered from some form of handicap or were emotionally disturbed. Most of them had been labelled by society as 'unemployable' and when they arrived, they had very little hope of ever finding full time work or even living independent lives. Yet, after a two year course here, working and learning through horses, the majority of them found employment and could lead useful lives.

Because the horse demands a disciplined routine, the students learned to structure their own lives to meet the needs of the horses and through them were motivated to learn new skills which prepared them for coping with life outside the Centre.

It was lovely to see these young people with the horses, handling them with confidence and affection. As Don had so rightly said, these teenagers were responding to horses in a way that they might never have responded to a human, and we were told that horsemastership was not the only thing they learnt here. A 'Further Education through Horsemastership Course' included banking, health care and social skills, through which they developed a respect for the needs of others and built up their own self-esteem.

I came away with my mind buzzing with ideas. But what interested me more than anything was a course which was run for young people who wanted to qualify to work with these handicapped youngsters.

When I reached home, the family were having supper and I told them how it was that horses could be used to help these people so that, instead of being social outcasts, after working and learning through horses under the supervision of dedicated teachers, they became useful members of society.

I went on to tell them about the course they ran to train young people in riding therapy and the educational use of horses.

'I'd love to do that course,' I said.

'How long does it last?' asked Dad.

'There's a Foundation Course which lasts a year and is divided into three terms. It also includes training for the British Horse Society's Assistant Instructor's Certificate.'

'That sounds a good idea,' said Dad. 'Gives you some sort of qualification. Have you any idea of the cost?'

'No, but it's probably expensive unless it's possible to get a grant.'

'If it's something you really want to do,' said Dad, 'I think we could raise the money, even if we have to borrow it. It sounds as if you have given up the idea of buying a horse for the moment and this seems to me to be something far more practical and useful.' He looked across the table at Mum and she nodded in agreement. 'After all,' he went on, 'we owe you something for all the work you've put in on the farm this summer.'

'Dad, I don't want payment for it.'

'I know you don't, but if this is something you're interested in, I think you should go ahead with it. Perhaps you'd better get in touch with them and find out more about it.'

'I'll ring and ask them to send me the information,' I

said. 'Dad, would you and Philip be able to manage if I left fairly soon?'

I glanced at Phil. He had, after all, given up the idea of an agricultural college for the time being because we couldn't afford it. How would he feel about this training?

'I think you should go ahead,' he said, generously. 'We can manage and if you're going on with this special riding for children, you need more experience and proper qualifications and that means training. What are you doing about the children when you're away? I suppose you'll have to close it down.'

I hadn't thought it through yet. I had an idea that if I went away to work, I'd come home at week-ends but now it would be more like school terms. 'I'm sure the others will want to keep it going, especially Mrs Owen. She was fascinated by the idea. Besides I'll be home for the holidays and I can help then.'

When I rang the Centre, they told me that before I could be accepted for the course, I would have to complete a five-day residential trial period to see if I was suitable. I had no reservations as I filled in the form and sent in my application. My only fear was that they wouldn't take me, but when I thought it over, I was pretty sure that I had the right qualifications.

One evening just before I left, Phil had gone to see Kirsty and I was in my old jeans and jacket, feeding the pigs for him. I suddenly looked up to find Matthew standing there watching me. I hadn't seen much of him lately because Dad was now back on light work, we were managing quite well and there was no need for him to come over. But we had been to the cinema together and I had told him about Bruce's offer. I wasn't surprised he

125

was against it. He didn't like Bruce.

'I don't think you'd be happy there,' he had said. 'It led to all sorts of problems, didn't it?' I knew he was thinking about the day of Dad's accident and all that led up to it.

Now I felt rather embarrassed. I looked an awful mess with my hair all over the place and gumboots deep in dirt. I had just come out of the pens, having poured the swill into the troughs, and the noise from the pigs was deafening. Matthew took the bucket from me and put it on the ground.

'You've caught me at an awkward moment,' I said with a grin.

'You look great, Paula. I love you like that.'

I looked at him. He must be joking, but his eyes were serious. 'Actually, I came over because I have something to tell you,' he said.

I waited and he went on, 'My father's decided to hand over a hundred acres of land so that I can farm it myself. He wants to cut down a bit, and we've been thinking about converting a derelict cottage nearby, so that eventually I can have my own place. It would be a good investment.'

'That's great, Matthew.'

'Paula, would you consider marrying a farmer?'

I hesitated. Matthew was always taking me by surprise.

'I'm going away, Matthew.'

'Going away?' He was clearly puzzled. 'Why didn't you tell me?'

'I've only just decided. I'm going to take a course in Riding Therapy in the New Forest.' I began to tell him about it, but he didn't seem to be listening.

'How long is this going to last?'

'A year. I shall come home for the holidays and help with the children here. It's something I really want to do. When I'm qualified I'll be in a much better position to help them and I might be able to develop it. It was incredible how I heard about it, Matthew.'

I told him about the TV programme and how it had come just at a time when I was trying to make up my mind what to do.

'It's amazing how, if we ask, we're given guidance at precisely the right time,' I said.

He grinned then. 'In that case you're right to go ahead with it,' he said, 'but I'm going to miss you. When are you leaving?'

'In a week's time.'

'Well then, perhaps it's just as well. I can get things organised without distractions.' His brown eyes gently teased me. 'But once I get sorted out, I can promise you a place for your riding school.'

'Matthew, please give me time. I don't want to be tied by promises. Not yet. I want to go away and concentrate on this course. The only thing I'm sure about at the moment is that I want to help these kids. That's enough for now.'

'I'm happy to wait,' said Matthew, cheerfully. 'I love you and I'm confident that the time will come when you'll give me the answer I'm waiting for.' Then he took me in his arms and gave me a long kiss.

As usual he was right, I thought, settling happily in his arms. One day I'd probably be back into farming again, but then it would be with Matthew and together we would make plans for the future.